Condemned To Be

A collection of short stories

by

Stephen Howard

Contents

Replicas

Stack the tins on the shelf, push the furthest sell-by dates to the back. Seventy-four years from now.

Continue with protocol.

Tom is stacking the shelf further down the aisle. Tom is my replica in every way. Lab 17 – outlying Manchester district lab. I stack more tins, dates of seventy-three years, place them in middle of shelf. An elderly woman pushes her trolley to the top of the aisle, spies Tom and I, hastily shuffles along to the next aisle. Her face is hidden, regulation surgical mask.

Tom and I don't require surgical masks. This sets us apart. As do our designated Red Shirts.

The fan whirls above us, a sickly whirring noise. Makes Tom queasy, also. We are identical in every way. I see Tom stack his shelf, notice our smooth movements in sync. Tom looks up too, smiles at me. Noticed the same thing, no doubt. Identical in every way.

Working day ends at 18:00. Tom and I walk home, past the Trafford Centre, under the M60 motorway bridge, past Trafford Retail Park with its multiplex of restaurants and discount clothing stores, and turn right, past the high bushes concealing the lorry lane, into our apartment complex. The complex design is the much-maligned brutalist style, considered quite the eyesore. Tom and I say it has charm. It is a clone complex. Deliberate design of low status. Severe concrete steps lead up to the entrance.

Walk down the sterile corridor, stop at the window to receive our dinner packs from the masked porter – eyes greet us with daily dose of suspicion and mistrust. Lift at end of the corridor, two potted plants beside it, takes us up to our apartment.

Evening television begins 19:00, several television programmes play back-to-back until 22.00. Then it's time to go to bed. Tom and I sit at our dinner table, open our packs. Fish pie and assorted vegetables in separate repositories.

"I don't think they like us, do they Tim?" says Tom, pausing between bites. Insouciant, he continues eating.

"At least they leave us alone," I reply. This again.

"That woman ran away earlier. If we weren't identical, if there was just one of us, wearing a surgical mask, and no Red Shirt, she wouldn't run away."

Cars driving round the Nag's Head Circle Roundabout outside, exhausts sputtering. Cars are produced on a manufacturing line, one after another. Tom's pale plain face is identical to mine. Now it appears different. Overnight, Tom drifted away and was replaced with someone new. Which is the identity inhabiting Tom?

"Would you like some air, Tom? We could go up to the rooftop garden. There's enough time before evening television begins," I say. Stand up, leave remains of meal. Tom stands. The lift takes us to the roof. All around are sloped tiled roofs of houses. Public House, a large old building, sits across from us. Clone complexes punctuate the skyline, identical in almost every way to this one, standing tall. Low and flimsy translucent layer of something sits beneath the clouds above. Weathervane spins scratchily in the wind. The rooftop garden is one place we are allowed to add something different and decorative to the building. Tom and I chose two stone gargoyle heads.

Walk to edge of the roof, past small trees, bushes, and flowers, lean over. Directly below, concrete steps up to front entrance. Tom stood beside me, looks ahead. A smile on his face.

"You're right, Tom... If there were one of us, we could blend in, a clone among natural humans. But to what end?" I ask. We face each other.

"Don't you want more from existence, Tim? Look at us. We can walk about outside. We don't have to wear masks. The sickness won't affect us. Why are we treated like lower class people? Why do people turn away just because we came from a lab?" Tom pleads. Earnestness in expression. And pain. For too long. Place my arm on Tom's shoulder. A chagrined smile on his face. Tom turns, faces murky, pink horizon. I step back.

"What do you see, Tom?" I ask. Edge further back. Two identical stone gargoyles, ours, sit side-by-side before thorny garden bushes.

"Pollution. But nice colours. And possibilities. No more stacking shelves."

We are identical in every way. By design, our fate is shared. That is why we were created, that is how we are viewed, that is what we are.

Stone gargoyle brought down out of air, onto Tom's head. Limp body falls over side, pink murky sky ahead of me. Look down. Dark stain spreads from head onto grey-stone steps. Possibilities, right. For me.

Humanity and the Wall

They were baying at the bricks below. Shah spat down upon the mob and shifted his rifle upon his shoulder. "Mindless zombies," he muttered.

North of the wall was desolate and grey-scorched, as if the fires of hell had burst forth from their beleaguered cage beneath this plane of existence. Blackened trees crumbled in the wind, mounds of earth and dirt rose and fell about the land, towns and cities were deserted; neglect and contempt hung on the air. What was left of the people had banded together, smelling ripe flesh beyond the wall – they lusted for human meat – and moaned endlessly, clawing at the barrier between them and sustenance.

"Do you wonder why we still man the wall, Shah?" asked Ron. Eyes closed, he smelt the air facing south. He turned back to face the south.

"Do you ever pay attention, Ron? Sometimes I think you oughtta be down there, spitting froth from your mouth and banging at the wall, wailing senselessly. We gotta watch for any change in behaviour. If they start to get smart, or start tryna find a way through besides headfirst, then we gotta report it to the boss who sends it onto headquarters who forward it to the capital and then who knows who's involved but I sure as hell don't wanna speak to them," said Shah, spitting over the side again. "Got one," he grinned.

Ron stayed quiet. Shah's ranting is tiresome, he thought. I ask a simple question and suddenly it's time to call me an idiot again. All Shah does is repeat what he's been told over and over again until it's ingrained in his mind and when someone disagrees with his predetermined logic they're automatically an idiot. His problem is he doesn't question anything he's told. Ron looked up to see a flock of seagulls flying southwards. They passed from the spore-tinged bleak sky of the north into the pale blue lucidity of the southern sky, the strain upon their wings easing as they did, as if the strain dissipated upon crossing the divide. Ron's gaze was drawn now to the verdant fields and the blossoming rose bushes and the enormous towering oaks. Beneath them, emerging from the shrubbery at the foot of the wall, was a lovely brown rabbit. Ron smiled, watching it closely. It poked its head out to begin with, smelling the fresh, inviting air. It became brave and began to skip out into the safety of the open field. Ron saw a peripheral glint to his right. A sharp crack and a burst of red upon the lush green grass. There was a final twitch and then it was still. A wad of spit plunged through the air. "Got it," Shah grinned, pulling his rifle back onto his shoulder.

The wailing on the north side of the wall rose briefly with the loud noise of the gun shot. The zombies rallied, flinging themselves with fresh verve at the wall. Shah poked his head over the north side and pulled his rifle off his shoulders again, taking aim. There was a sharp crack once more. A sharp intake of breath. Then Shah fell over the parapet, onto the north side, to be torn apart by ravenous zombies. If you feed them once in a while, they'll keep quiet, thought Ron, holstering his pistol.

The Bus Show

Round and round they go. The wheels on the bus. And the whole cast are here. The tall woman who always wears a hat, no matter the weather. The grizzled man in a mucky high vis jacket. The young kid who sits there rocking back and forth, ready to leap off the bus the second the doors open at his stop. And the red-haired girl with the black and white chessboard backpack. There are a few others, mostly students who'd get off the bus before it had even left town, but I won't tell you about them all. They're always on the 18:02 from the bus station in town, always quietly staring at the congested scenery through the windows, thinning bit by tedious bit as the bus whistles by. And I bet they knew me. Always sits at the back, in the corner, wishing to be left alone, ostentatious headphones wrapped around his ears like a medieval torture device. That's me, alright. Part of the cast. I had a view of the whole bus, a dark tunnel of chewing gum-studded seats and adverts for TV shows that finished airing a year ago or more.

It's why I knew every regular face on that bus.

It's why I realised when, one by one, they started disappearing.

*

She was first to go, of course. The red-haired girl. I'll admit, I always noticed her. Call it a little crush. I thought she was cute. So when she wasn't on the bus, I noticed. I was disappointed when she didn't get on that first time because each new day was going to be the day I'd sit next to her and start a conversation. I guess I missed my stop.

You might be thinking, well, people change their routine all the time. A new job, a new contract, bought a car, started taking the train, gone out for a drink after work, and so on. But I had this unsettling feeling in my stomach even on the first day she wasn't on the bus. Our little ecosystem had suffered a schism. It wasn't natural. And when the natural balance is disturbed, disturbing things will often take place.

For a few days I sat in my corner seat and gazed at the empty places on the bus, picturing red hair spilling down upon a chessboard, tilting to the left or right spasmodically, bobbing up and down with the rhythm of the bus. Despite the freeing up of space one less person created, it seemed to have the opposite effect. The dark tunnel of the bus before me seemed just a little darker, just a little smaller.

It was a few nights later, watching the news, that our little world darkened further.

*

A missing person report oozed from the television like blood from a wound, gushing, desperate. Last spotted outside here, a picture of the place, if you saw or heard anything please report it, and so on. A standard report, concise. Beneath the words, I felt, something more sinister. I knew the restaurant, a Chinese place the bus drove past about 27 minutes into its route. It was deeply strange that these were the circumstances, a missing person report, under which I learned her name. She was 24 years of age. It was a report lacking in detail, like the vague school reports of your youth, where the reporter knows few real details about the person. I guess that meant the police were clueless so far. I tried to think, but I could only remember her getting off at her stop alone, as always, and trudging back past my window as the bus drove off. There was nothing I could think of out of the ordinary, nothing of note. My observations were as inconsequential as the concept of the value of human life was to a murderer. I hoped the worst had not happened.

In the meantime, the wheels on the bus kept spinning, round and round. Day after day. I settled back into the routine, but the bus felt smaller, tighter, like a piece of clothing that no longer fit. I couldn't be sure how much time had passed without seeing any reports indicating she'd been located. Is no news truly good news? I'd venture not. It's a state of limbo, of purgatory, with no end in sight.

After I'd given up on hearing any news, our little world grew even smaller. The tall woman who always wore a hat stopped getting on the bus. She was always smartly dressed, but a little old-fashioned. I expect she was someone's slightly embarrassing but thoroughly respectable mum. A strong sense of despair gripped me that first time I noticed she wasn't on the bus. I began to wonder whether anyone else was noticing this second disappearance and linking it to the first, but I could hardly make this conversation the first I'd had with a fellow passenger, so I didn't pursue it. Instead, I started to give greater thought to the blackouts I'd been having.

*

I can't remember the first time I had a blackout. I call them blackouts, but I don't know if that's technically correct for what I've been experiencing. I looked online and blackouts are linked to psychogenic seizures or high alcohol consumption. These didn't seem likely. I enjoy a drink, but I'm not throwing back 14 units a night, that's for sure. So for some other reason which, as of yet, is unexplained, my hippocampus is taking long relaxing breaks and I'm struggling to fill in long periods of the unknown.

It was hard to notice at first, almost as if I'd taken a long nap. But then they'd happen during work and a whole afternoon would disappear. Ostensibly, I'd continued functioning. Inwardly, I was asleep. It didn't make sense. I didn't like doctors though, with their condescending tone and shiny Mercedes in the car park, so I hadn't been to see one yet. All I could say with certainty was I'd been experiencing blackouts, periods of time where I'm floating on a different plane, some other level of existence, while my physical body continued to function, and this had been going on for at least two months, but maybe longer. It was deeply troubling.

Now I guess you can see where I'm going with this. I can't account for my whereabouts or actions for prolonged periods, and the cast members in my bus journey home from work have begun to disappear. I'm starting to worry I'm involved. I'm losing track of the timeline. When exactly did the red-haired girl go missing?

When did the tall woman who always wore a hat go missing? I can't be sure of where I was and my blackouts are becoming more and more frequent.

*

I'm in my kitchen, a small square with the usual white goods. Pine cupboards surrounded me like a dense, benign forest. I'm cutting potatoes into even pieces and putting them into boiling water. I've already wrapped the chicken fillet in bacon, then wrapped it in foil so it looks like a conspiracy theorist's hat. I turn the fan on above the oven and leave the potatoes in the steaming pan. The radio is playing in the background, *I Wanna Be Adored* by The Stone Roses. A good song. But the radio is making occasional scratchy noises. I can never seem to tune it perfectly to the station. As I flick the kettle on (I always enjoy a cup of tea while my dinner is cooking) there's a local news bulletin. Another missing person report. There's no physical description but I know in my bones how it should read: a tall woman, always wearing a hat, smartly dressed if a little old-fashioned, looks like someone's slightly embarrassing mum. They read out her name. It suited her well. And the investigation is ongoing. No reason so far to link it to the recent case of the young red-haired woman. I suspected otherwise.

Tea bag in mug, one sugar, pour the water, squeeze the bag, remove, pour in milk, stir. I sat down for a minute on my sofa, the leather squelching beneath me, and I gazed out of the south-facing window. Clouds drifted by, clouds with that ever-so-slightly darkened outline of oncoming evening. I could hear the wheels of the bus turning, like big lumps of rock tumbling down a steep hill.

Sisyphus tries to roll them back up, but they're forever tumbling down. In the clouds I can see the grotesque faces of the missing women, but they appear lifeless and disturbed. Is this my imagination running wild, or have I seen the faces in this state already? I sip my tea, stand up, and attend to my dinner.

*

There are growing purple bags beneath my eyes. I pick up my electronic shaver and go to work on my face, hyper-aware how many years my facial hair adds. It resembles a garden left uncut, growing awkwardly, unkempt and wild. You can't see what lurks beneath the grass. I wash the sink of hair afterwards and wash myself up.

I almost resemble a human being now.

For the next several hours I try to read, hoping it will send me to sleep. *Kafka by the Shore*, by Murakami, if you were wondering. I usually devour his work, but I can't concentrate. Listless, forlorn, a heavy weight rests within my chest. I keep thinking of the red-haired girl, and the tall woman who likes to wear hats, and wondering how many people are missing them now. Lots, I imagine. The red-haired girl probably had a boyfriend, and a big group of friends she's had since school. And a pet cat called Meredith, or Zippo. The tall woman no doubt had a husband and a son, an accountant and a student, who are now left to fumble through the darkness on their own. It's several hours before I fall asleep, the emptiness of my apartment finally engulfing me like a blue whale swallowing krill.

*

The journey home from work seemed to change very little over the next few days. No one else noticed the growing emptiness, the wheels continued to turn, round and round they went, round and round we went. The young lad, who would always sit near the front, continued to rock back and forth as if he were about to lunge for something, and the man in the high vis jacket, unshaven and gaunt, would casually lean against the wall, gazing aimlessly out the window. Their behaviour seemed not to have altered, as if nothing had changed. Was it simply I who registered the loss of our fellow cast members?

It had grown darker, and rain spattered the bus windows like a colourless Jackson Pollock. Trails of water crept through the edges of the panes of glass, like soldiers infiltrating an enemy fortress. I wiped away the condensation on the glass with my finger and was faced with my reflection. The face was grotesque and inhabited by an unnatural fear. I turned away sharply and looked down the bus, the dark tunnel with only two others occupying it. The little world of the 18:02 from town had shrunk further.

The next day the world shrank again. The young man who rocked back and forth failed to get on the bus. He had disappeared. And, worse still, I had blacked out for the entire evening.

*

I could no longer see any other link to these disappearances beyond the 18:02. And I began to wonder whether I should stay home from work, or go to see the doctor, or even the police. Am I dangerous? Am I even responsible? Am I in danger? I couldn't say. The disappearances had happened in a particular order. From least threatening, from a physical standpoint, onwards. First the young girl, then the older, taller woman. Then the young man. A calculated rise in difficulty. If I was the malevolent force behind the disappearances, that's the order I'd have chosen. The thought made me sick.

Despite my reservations, I had a feeling I needed to continue with my life, stick to my routine, and wait for something to happen. Of the regulars on the 18:02 from town, only the man in the high vis jacket and I remained. The handful of students would filter off after only a few stops. Once the bus left town it was just the regulars again.

And that's where I am now.

The tall red brick buildings, the noisy colours of the mega brand stores, all slide away.

And then everything else, too.

I'm walking down an alleyway, which looks to be a cut-through behind a few restaurants and stores. There's steam rising from vents and large commercial bins dotted about, surrounded by black bin bags. I don't recognise this alley. This isn't my route home.

And I can hear someone humming. It's a familiar tune. Round and round they go. The wheels on the bus. The wheels on the bus go round and round, round and round, round and round. He walks around the corner casually, the same nonchalance with which he leans against the window on the bus. In this dark alley, the high vis jacket shines eerily. High vis jacket man has followed me down this alley.

"Round and round they go," he said, smiling. His voice is deep, with the hoarse tone of a smoker. "It was strange, following you just now. Like you weren't really here. Or rather you were, but someone else was controlling you. But it made following you very easy. You were oblivious."

He continued walking toward me, and I stood still, watching him. A cat darted out from behind a pile of bin bags and disappeared around the corner. Drowning engine noises barely reached us from the street.

"I can hear the misery around me, the loneliness, the pain. People who are crying out for it all to end. I facilitate that ending. I can take away the pain. Do you want me to take away the pain?"

He was stood about five paces from me, hardly blinking, his eyes fixed upon me. There was a strange power behind them, something unnatural. I could sense the weight of his presence, as if I were Atlas holding the world up upon my shoulders. I tried to focus on his words.

"What do you mean, you 'facilitate that ending'?" I asked.

"That's simple," he replied, "in return for your co-operation, I can lift and store your pain elsewhere. That is, I can transfer it to a new host, someone more... deserving. They must then live with the pain." He took a step closer to me. His jacket shimmered as a light came on above a door to his left, motion activated, no doubt.

"But people have been disappearing. What's the catch?" I ask. For the first time, a shiver runs through me, as if we're reaching the climax of our encounter.

"For some people, you take away their pain and you take away too much of them. Without the pain and everything it entails, they're no longer... living. They simply fade away. It's what I suppose in my line of work we call a *condition. If the person's natural balance, their natural eco-system, is disturbed too greatly, then the person will simply cease to function. The *condition is the risk you have to take for releasing all of your pain. It's just another business transaction in our capitalist society. Plenty of people end up just fine, believe me," he added, a yellow grin stretching across his face. A heavy smoker, I assume. He took a step closer. His eyes narrowed, expecting an answer.

I thought about the emptiness of my apartment. The dark tunnel of the bus, and the secret world I had created, the cast of characters on my journey home. I thought about my blackouts, the cessation of self-control for long periods, the absence of memory. Everything was just a show, a façade. Beneath it all there was... what? I couldn't say.

Despite all of this, it was bearable. It was simply existence and all it encompassed. I mean, it's what we all have to face, isn't it?

I turned to look him in the eye and gave him my answer.

*

The students were unusually noisy today, gabbling like penguins at the front of the bus. I closed my eyes to drown them out. I counted the minutes until they departed and it was just the usual 18:02 from town crowd. Not that we could be classed as a crowd anymore.

I opened my eyes.

And there they were. The young lad, rocking back and forth on his seat near the front. The tall woman, wearing a striking Russian ushanka, and the red-haired girl, sat still wearing her chessboard backpack. Where was the facilitator?

"Surprised," said a voice to my right, giving me a fright in the process. I turned and was faced with a wide yellow grin.

"But… how?" was about all I could muster.

"Sometimes it takes people a little while to find the right balance," he said. "Their families were all very worried and very happy to have them back. These little mysteries happen, after all. A short period trapped in limbo. Most make it back. Most people carry a normal amount of pain. But if you carry a lot of pain and try to release it all at once… well, it's difficult to cope. You see, the balance of life isn't just pain or joy. It's far more complex, and a heck of a lot of ingredients are mixed in the pot. You need an outlet for pain, otherwise it just builds and builds. Simplistically, think of it like a volcano, working towards explosion. The pressure is similar in life. Don't let it build, don't take it all on on your own. That's a recipe for disaster. And remember, whatever is happening on the surface is just for show, there's plenty more going on below."

I ran the words through my mind, trying to read between the lines. I gazed at them all, unsure how the cast had been brought back together. The right balance? An outlet for pain? I focused my gaze upon the girl with the red hair. It poured down her backpack like molten lava, shimmering ethereally. I looked to my right, at the facilitator, sat by me in his high vis jacket.

"Why a bus?" I asked, curious.

"I work in places where the aura of pain is stronger, where it's acutely felt," he said in a steady tone.

Fair enough.

19

I stood up and moved past him, to walk down the dark tunnel, my earphones hanging around my neck like a lead weight. The seat by the 24-year-old, red-haired young woman was empty. Behind me, I heard someone humming. The wheels on the bus go round and round. I smiled and continued on. I asked if I could take the spare seat.

The Sea, the Darkness

I could see the waters billowing in the distance on the starboard side. Sea water and foam spilt upon the deck. The captain lay motionless, pale, dead. Blood seeped from the back of his head, diluting the water already on-deck, then soaking into the wooden panels. It joined the collage of blackened blood stains, each a separate memory of a separate man and a separate death. The rogue mast had rolled away but slid back and forth like a rum drunk as the ship rocked in the heavy waves. Wind whipped up from all angles. Darkness engulfed the ship, as, soon enough, would the sea.

*

Many of the vessels lined up in the harbour were in a state of disrepair. Mists from the sea drifted between them, rising from the still, cold water and bringing that familiar taste of brine. Our age of piracy was dying. The British fleet, amongst others, commanded the seas now. Men who once would have given their lives for the pursuit of piracy were now enlisted under the King's name. Corsair ships roamed the Mediterranean but had crusades of their own or money from the French or

Spanish. The pirate way had all but disappeared. Even Teach was dead, his body reduced to sediment, his head a mere trophy. I had begun to feel like one of the ancient relics Kidd had buried in obscure spots on islands around the globe: lost.

Men roamed the harbour, singing the old songs, with drink spilled down their shirts. I still enjoyed hearing the ditties, but the heart was gone from them. These lads knew the words, but not where they came from or what they meant. These people were playing the role, not inhabiting it, living it. I question what I myself have become. Even as I stare out to sea, memories flood forth of paintings hung in captain's quarters – I have become a parody too. The gulls cry overhead.

A respectable young couple, a gentleman and a lady holding a parasol, stroll calmly along the promenade, chortling and smiling. No one pays them any attention and they stroll on insouciant and happy. The cold begins to set in again. Old bones are more easily infected with it, you see. The Old Sea Dog's tavern sign is swinging gently in the wind, until a more violent gust causes it to rattle, its rusty chain spitting minute flecks of shrapnel.

Within the alcove of the door hangs a mirror with a small crack in the top right corner. I see a sad, roughly hewn face looking out; its grey beard slightly matted, its nose crooked. The mouth is a bit lop-sided, a small scar trailing from the corner, much like that of a fish that has been hooked and thrown back into the sea. I ducked under the low door. Merriment and mirth greeted me. A man I had never seen before declared it was a good evening and stumbled past, his arm around a young woman. Glasses banged upon tables and the air was littered with swears and curses. Torches adorned the walls. For one sudden, violent moment they seemed to flicker in unison and a morbid silence gripped the room. I looked around, but no one seemed perturbed. I shook my head and ordered a drink.

The barman expressed some interest in a conversation, but I felt too inclined to introversion to make the effort tonight. As with most barmen, he failed to sense this. He'd been alone a long time, his wife having died some years ago. One day she walked straight out of the tavern and carried on into the sea. Never came back. I leant him an ear from time to time, but not tonight. I tossed him a coin and turned away. Heat came over me in waves. Too many people were crowded together so I hurried toward a more secluded corner. Spotting a spare seat, I made my way over. A girl sat across from it. She seemed to be alone. And young. Long black hair failed to conceal a pair of gold earrings. Her fingers were dressed in several rings. Obviously, she wasn't a regular – possibly she was a traveller. The light around her appeared to shrink, as if battling the darkness for territory. I could detect an odour, heavy and intoxicating, and somewhat familiar. Acting against a strong feeling I had to find another seat, I approached her. Her eyes flickered about, distracted, as though each of the voices in the room were speaking to her privately and she knew not who to turn to.

"Evening, lass," I said as I took the seat opposite her and placed my drink on the chipped, dark wood table. Her eyes narrowed, shifting from my drink, to my attire, to my face.

"I'm not to be paid for, if that's what you're thinking," she declared, sitting back. Her voice was somewhat distant and scratchy with a hard-to-place accent, but her diction was lucid. Certainly, she wasn't a regular – no woman enters this place unless she anticipates being well paid. I thought about warning her she was best leaving now whilst she could. No one needs such hassle. But it struck me as odd that, in a place such as this, she remained sat alone and undisturbed until my arrival. No eyes rested on her, almost like no one could see she was there.

"It's not. I don't do that," I added, taking some of my drink. The taste was disgusting. Something swirled round the bottom of the glass. I took some more.

"No, I can see that. Probably because of her, I'm sure," said the girl. The smirk on her face aroused my suspicion further. She continued: "It's amazing to be in a room full of such remorse and pain. It's pitiable, and yet I feel none, for each man, haunted by whatever ghost is standing over his shoulder, each man has earned them. To a one. Violence pervades this room. It hangs over the sea as a thick mist, and you all rush into it knowing not what devil's agreement you are entering into. Yes, perhaps it is a pity, sometimes. You, for instance. Your ghost doesn't haunt you. She waits for you."

I sat opposite her in silence. At a glance, there wasn't a melancholy soul in the building, mirth and merriment the clear order of the day. But these are shallow passions, and the girl had identified this already. Knowledge is a powerful tool. In my world, it could be the difference between hostility and camaraderie, peace and mutiny. But what was such knowledge doing in a lass so young? Cries roused us briefly. A table overturned in the adjacent room. Card games often got out of hand. These men rarely had much money to their name, and what little they did have they wasted. I asked the girl her name, but she shook her head.

24

"There are depths to you that remain unexplored. Somewhere in this darkness lies something, and it's restless. I cannot see it in the sea of darkness and that is most unusual." The girl leant forward and squinted at me. I had never before believed I could be made to feel uncomfortable by a young girl, but it was as if she were taking a stroll through my mind and I were watching her from a great distance. The feeling was disconcerting, and I could see the amusement dancing upon her face like the war dance of some far-flung tribe.

"You will see her one more time before the end, Captain," she said. With this, she rose and began to drift from the room and toward the door. The crowd parted like an island inlet as she flowed forward and away, meandering out of my life. Whatever she had meant by her words she could not possibly be correct. Yet mystery is enticing. It is what leads a man toward the life I have lived. Mystery and an inability to do anything else. Or sorrow. Often, extreme sorrow is the reason a man spends his life at sea in the company of men and men alone. Even the ones who get away for a while drift back like flotsam or the deadwood of a wreck, dragged ceaselessly toward a lonely beach. It is no calling. It is a curse. A curse we all live with.

I rose and pushed past the crowd and exited.

The air was stiff and cold. I looked left and right, but the girl was gone. A young couple walked past, a young gentleman and a girl holding a parasol. They were giggling to themselves. The screech of the gulls above awakened me from whatever state into which I had drifted. Images flashed across my mind, trying to drag me into different times; some painful, some not. I looked upon the decaying ships in the harbour once more. The ships began to fade away before my eyes.

*

We lay upon the grass staring up at the clouds above. I heard a lyrical laugh and turned my neck to see her face. I could not tell what was more radiant: her face or the sun above. The only dark cloud on the horizon was my impending voyage with the merchant. But I could not escape my contract or my obligations. The sea was to be my escape. And then she arrived like a maelstrom, turning everything in my life upside down. Evangeline was the merchant's daughter, and a fine girl she was too. It was unlikely he'd take too kindly to my spending so much time with her, which made my parting with Evangeline necessary. If I could prove myself to the merchant, and perhaps prove to be a good suitor for his daughter, then we could be happy together. Staring up at the blue sky, the pleasant clouds drifting harmlessly across it, and looking across at Evangeline, I knew it was all going to work out. I just knew it.

Evangeline rose from the dry patch of grass and circled the meadow as I watched her. We had walked up from the town, away from prying eyes. A deer skirted around the edge of the meadow, around the edge of the light, wandering in the shadows. It spooked quite suddenly and sprinted off. Evangeline seemed preoccupied with the trees. She ran her hand down the creases in the bark. I asked her what it was that fascinated her about them. Evangeline said it was interesting how the trees wore their age just like humans, and how they seemed to be in such pain. Yew trees overlooked graveyards, she said, they stood guard over death itself. I did not understand this and had intended to ask her more, but she laughed and continued to stroll around the field. We are surrounded by yew trees, she shouted to me from across the meadow.

*

The harbour was thronging with people unloading the merchant's majestic ship; thick ropes tied it to the jetty. Hurried voices mixed with the clatter of loading and unloading ships, barrels being heaved and dropped carelessly, gulls uttering their jagged cries above. I gazed upon this entire sight with awe for I longed for my own seafaring adventure. Out at sea, the world must seem so uncomplicated, where you can listen to the waves and be alone with your thoughts. If I could convince a merchant to take me on as a cabin boy or a simple deckhand, I may realise my dreams.

I pushed through the crowd and knocked into a young girl. Her black hair half-covered her face, but I was sure I felt a burning rage flare ever so briefly. I could smell a thick perfume. A hand bearing several gold rings pushed her hair from her face as she stormed away. For a moment, I watched her go, but I turned back and made for the ship. A man in a rich, scarlet jacket and a fine silk shirt was crossing the walkway from the ship to the jetty in deep discussion with a man holding a scroll and a quill. I rushed up to him.

"Sir, may I be of assistance?" I declared, standing upright and fixing him with my best stare. The man with the scroll moved forward as if to intercept me, but a hand fell on his shoulder. The merchant smiled.

"I'm afraid not, young man. At least not for now. If

you attend the harbour office tomorrow morning you can place your name down for any future opportunities. There is a process in place, of course, but if you should succeed in interview, you can be of assistance in the future." He nodded once at me and went on his way, the other man leaving with him. I resolved immediately to go along to the office in the morning to do just as he had said. I stared out at the sea again. The morning sun caused it to glisten, the ripples of the waves somewhat brighter for it. I turned away to see which way the merchant had gone. He was not far ahead. He was now in deep discussion with a young woman. He glanced over his shoulder in my direction once before continuing on his way. The girl remained standing there for a moment. She too was looking towards me, a smile on her face. She was the most hauntingly beautiful girl I had ever laid eyes on.

*

The face in the mirror was haggard and unshaven – an uneven, dark stubble doing nothing to compliment the ominous shadows beneath my eyes. Clothes were splayed all around my room. I could hear noise from downstairs – laughter and mirth. But the rent was cheap and they didn't ask questions, so it would have to do. And anyway, they left me to myself. I poured another drink and walked toward the window. The moon appeared huge in the sky, highlighting the ripples of the waves of the sea. I wondered what lay beneath this shimmering surface. I clasped the letter tightly in my hand, before easing my grip and reading it once more.

Dearest Nathaniel,

By now you will know of my fate – the yew trees will watch over me. It may trouble you that I could not bear to continue living without you by my side. Please, try to let this go. The reasons I am to do this are manifold and are so complex that I cannot come to find the appropriate words for them. However, I will try to explain them as best I can in this letter. Just know, too, that my heart is yours, and it always will be. The first reason is one that hangs over me like a spectre; the thought of you being away at sea with father, not knowing whether either of you are safe or even alive, is too great a burden to carry. It slowly killed my mother; I saw every day how it haunted her, not knowing whether father would return. The second reason is less easy to explain. All I know, or all I can think to say or to describe it, is that it feels like a heavy weight has always hung around my neck like some great, cursed ornate pendant. There were times when it felt lighter, namely the times when I was with you. However, I have always felt its presence, and I have always felt so inextricably close to the idea of death because of it. This is all I can think to say. Please also know this: I am truly sorry.

Yours, always,
Evangeline

I had lost count of how many times I had now read and reread the letter. On our return, we had learned of what Evangeline had done. It made sense that she would write me a letter, though it pained me to know that this was the one thing she could not come to describe accurately in words. She was a wonderful writer. So accomplished, in fact, that a publisher had expressed an interest in her work. This was a rare honour; I couldn't think of many other women writing right now. And to learn that she had leapt into the sea from the lighthouse cliff, the horror of it tore me apart. I knew not what to do now. Evangeline's death would haunt me until my dying day.

*

When your time has passed, you try to hold onto the things you once had. In a way, everyone is haunted, but we seafaring folk perhaps even more so than others. We don't learn to live with our ghosts, we leave them ashore and take off for a while. It's not a healthy way to cope, but it's our way and we're nothing if not stubborn. I had written words to this effect in my diary. I had been writing a diary on and off for many, many years, although I had little talent as a writer. It was something of a promise I kept to myself. Each journey, I would retire to my cabin, the small luxury afforded to the captain, and sit at my desk and write. Perhaps one day I may even try to publish them as some sort of memoir. It may be the only way to leave something of myself behind.

*

I could hear the wind whipping the ship from all sides, and cries came from the deck. I rushed out of my cabin to find a scene of such great elemental struggle it could have been from the pages of the Holy Bible itself. My men rushing back and forth, attempting to secure the mast, trying to hold her steady, muscles straining as if they'd hooked a shark on their fishing rod. I looked out to the starboard side. The waves thronged violently like a baying mob, intent on malevolence, and rain lashed down upon us all. Hovering amongst the waves was a pale, sombre figure, water falling through her much like it might trickle through my fingers. This spectre of womanly shape loomed within the thrall of the irate sea as if it were a calm and clear day. She was the most hauntingly beautiful girl I had ever seen, and the sea had her now. She seemed to fade away before my very eyes, like ships in the night. I had a vague notion that someone was calling out to me. The sea, the darkness, something was calling me.

*

I could see the captain, face down and motionless upon the deck. I looked again to the starboard side. The memories were gradually coming back to me. All those years I had been haunted by many things. By the past. By myself. By the sea. And yet I'd borne it all only for it to catch up with me in the end, as ghosts often will if you fail to lay them to rest. The sea had her all along, and now it has me too.

A Rainy Day

The rain began to trace thin, vertical lines against the window. Before long the pattering noise had become a constant din. Typical. The weather had recently decided to serve as a grim reminder of the dreariness of my job. Today alone I'd been shouted at four times by faceless voices. I'm perfectly sane, thank you very much; I'm simply glued to a telephone all day long calling people in the coldest manner I can muster. This is what we call 'being professional'. And it may one day be the catalyst for driving me over the sanity line, head hanging out the window, cigar in mouth, sunglasses and sombrero covering my goggle-eyed face, a suitcase full of illegal hallucinogens on the backseat. Only time will tell.

"Same old, same old, eh Wilkins," said a voice to my left. Jim was poking his head over the cubicle divider. He never used my first name. Lately I found this irksome, though it wasn't a new development. I sometimes wonder whether Jim has forgotten my name but refuses to admit it. That would be very like him. Or perhaps he genuinely believes I am a man with only one name. And I wish he'd do up his top button, he's wearing a tie for God's sake. In reaching over the cubicle he dislodges my calendar and it comes perilously close to spilling my coffee. One day I'll roast his beans.

"Oh, hi Jim. Yes, I suppose," I reply, getting up slowly to pin my calendar back up and readjust the files on my desk. These are generally client lists. I refer to these as the lists of my tormentors, but only to myself. I don't believe my manager would approve of attaching resentful nicknames to the lists. Jack Alman calls his 'The Hit List' which I think sounds quite threatening really. Silent men in black suits and dark sunglasses will remove him one day and, frankly, we'll all be the better for it. If they do come for him, I'm taking his chair. Good lumbar support, doesn't squeak, a nice 360-degree spin; it's perfection. Bastard.

"Listen," Jim says conspiratorially, continuing to lean over the divider, proffering no apology, I note, for causing a mini-ruckus in my personal space. His expression screams: the following combination of words I am about to utter will change your life in a revelatory fashion.

"A few of us are heading for a drink after work. Even the new girl's coming. You in?"

Mind-blowing. We've been here before. Today is pay day. Every pay day, without fail, Jim insists that we immediately throw a severe chunk of it away at the pub. I know he won't take no for an answer, which is probably why he has held a job in telesales. I can handle one drink; God knows I'll need it before the day is over. In this job I'm always one shot of tequila away from an existential crisis. If nothing I do here is imbued with meaning, and I assure you it isn't, then what is the point of this colourless existence? I can't imagine Jim is the man for a philosophical exploration of what we're doing with our lives. I return to his question and the nauseating realisation that I can only answer in one way. "Yeah, sure," I say. After droning on about the new girl and offering an unwanted breakdown of her various body parts he finally disappears. I take a hefty gulp of my coffee. "Not strong enough," I mutter. The calendar is still off-centre. The word payday is scrawled by this date. The other days are largely blank.

*

The rain hasn't ceased as we head to the bar by the train station. It's the usual crowd heading out. They're okay, a bit loud and crude perhaps, but bearable company.

Stepping out into the street through the revolving glass door I remember there was no sign of rain this morning and I'd left my jacket and umbrella at home. I'm always doing this. Damn. I brace myself for the tirade of water when there's a clicking noise beside me. A girl is holding an umbrella. I don't recognise her. She reaches to cover me too.

"I take it you don't pay much attention to the weather reports?" she says, smiling at me with raised eyebrows. She must be the new girl Jim mentioned.

"No, I guess I'm just one of life's risk takers," I say, slightly taken aback at my own light-heartedness. It surprises me further to hear her laugh in response.

We exchange small talk during the short stroll up the road. Small talk is usually excruciatingly awkward and dull, but I find myself curious for a change. Her name is Lily. I like the name Lily. I was quite relieved she didn't have one of those silly names that celebrities call their kids. I don't think I could hold a conversation, or even take someone seriously, if they were called Magenta Apple Crumble.

"I've only been in the city two months," she says, awkwardly avoiding a puddle. "Everything is so big and loud."

"You get used to Jim," I respond, to which she laughs.

"He's quite something, eh? I was beginning to think I'd get the sack if I didn't agree to join everyone for a drink. Apparently, I have to hear Smithy's story about the swimming pool?"

I grimace. Not the swimming pool, not again.

"I'd hate to spoil it for you. My only advice would be, if he starts telling it, ignore everything he says until he seems to have finished, laugh, and hope he goes away."

We reach the bar laughing in our own little world and I thank her for allowing me to share her umbrella. I'd be dripping wet and grumpy had she not helped me, which I explain quite seriously, much to her amusement. We could still hear the rumbling of thunder and pitter patter of rain from downstairs; the bar is what was the old station workers' quarters. Dark wood, the all-round bar set in the middle, with large booths along each wall, and a low ceiling. Pleasantly decorated, no big-screen TVs, quite restrained by modern standards.

I passed Lily back her umbrella. Halfway along the road I took over holding it; she's a few inches shorter than me; her hair would barely tickle my chin. Anyway, I felt like I was inconveniencing her by allowing her to stretch to include me. Suddenly, I receive a slap on the back. It's Jim. I'd almost forgotten anyone else was with us.

"First round is on me," he declares. Jim always buys first round, it's his way of ensuring we stay late:

everyone's obliged to get a round in after he begins the process.

We settle into a booth and Lily sits down next to me. She smiles warmly and I smile back. I notice a couple of the other guys are paying her close attention. This doesn't surprise me. I realise now that she is very attractive. She has long blonde hair, blue eyes and full lips. Perhaps I hadn't consciously qualified this in my mind because I've been slowly disengaging with the world around me. It's easily done in the repetitive day-to-day. Back to Lily. She also has a tiny mole on her left cheek. I wonder if it's one of those beauty spots that girls draw on and is rarely in the same place from one day to the next. I decide it would be inappropriate to ask – I don't even know if that's a real thing. But now I'm worried I'm focusing on her looks too much. Am I objectifying her? I've been reading a lot of articles lately in between half-hearted attempts at doing my job. And in-between checking the county cricket scores.

"Hey, Wilkins," someone shouts, "give us a hand with the drinks." It's Jim again. His request seems unusual as I'm sat in the middle. I decide he's just being awkward, but I'm grateful to be pulled from my thoughts. I almost go flying as I stumble past people to get out. I finally struggle free and reach the bar.

"Cheers mate," says Jim, "I can't be fussed carrying them all on a tray, it just looks daft." I nod in agreement. I rarely agree with Jim on anything because his opinions are usually stupid. I think he deliberately states the opposite of what he really believes sometimes just to be difficult. Either that or he's as disengaged with the world as I am but blissfully unaware of it.

"Hey, between you and me, Smithy's going to try and

chat up the newbie, so I thought I'd sit 'em next to each other. Here you go pal." He winks and hands me a couple of drinks and we head back to the booth. I guess I shouldn't be surprised, Smithy is always bragging about women. He claims to have slept with a minor celebrity, one of those reality show ones, but I'm not sure I believe him. Part of the claim was being forced to sign a contract declaring he wouldn't sell the story to the newspapers, which just can't be true; I'm not sure Smithy could even spell his own name. Smithy is that person in the office who always walks everywhere very fast, as if his time is of the utmost importance. He has strides like a gazelle but the grace of an orang-utan. It occurs to me I'm being unfair to orang-utans.

I'm sat across from Lily now. I think for one brief moment, when Smithy has his back turned, she glances at me and pulls a face, but I'm probably mistaken. It begins to occur to me that Jim didn't contemplate that I may have been 'chatting her up'. Never mind. It's not like he's wrong. I take a swig of my drink and start to half listen in on the insipid conversation Jim is having with Fran and Peter about holiday destinations. The rain always brings about conversations involving holidays.

"I'd recommend the Maldives," says Jim, "very nice this time of year, lovely beaches." Very nice Jim, I'm sure. And if Fran and Peter sell a kidney each they might be able to afford to get there.

The next couple of hours pass by uneventfully. Once or twice Lily pulls the same face I thought I saw earlier, I don't think she's enjoying having Smithy slobbering in her ear. It looks like he thinks she's deaf and he has to speak as close to her ear as possible to be heard. Anyway, I find I feel quite pleased that she isn't enjoying his company. I shouldn't revel in this, of course, but there's something about watching his type fail, after all the bragging, which feels quite joyous.

We have a few more drinks but I refrain after a while. I notice Lily too has slowed down. We don't have any further opportunity to talk, at least not properly. Smithy occupies her attention and I find this annoys me a great deal, even if she isn't happy about it. In fact, it actually seems worse that she's unhappy about it. I don't really give any consideration to what this means. Some more time passes and finally I decide to leave.

"Oh come on Wilkins," Jim shouts merrily, "you still owe us a round you bum, I'm not letting you off the hook that easily!"

"Oh yeah, here, next one is on me." I throw a twenty onto the table as I stand up.

"Come on man, have one more with us!" Jim declares with an air of finality.

"No, really, I've got to be up quite early, I promised to take my mum to my auntie's." This is a lie; I just want to leave at this point. I figure if I say it's for my mum he'll leave it, and I'm right. He shrugs and grabs the twenty from the table.

I make my goodbyes to the group and head for the door. I deliberately avoid singling out Lily; I don't quite know why. It's been an odd sort of day. I wave goodbye to everyone as a group and nothing more. I walk up the stairs, reach the door, and hesitate.

"Brilliant," I mutter. It's still raining heavily, but now I have no umbrella. I open the door and begin to step out when I hear someone coming up the stairs. I stop to hold the door; I hate it when people don't hold doors for others.

"I'm glad I caught you, I'd hate for you to get soaked now after I tried so hard to keep you dry." It's Lily. She smiles warmly and I smile back.

"No, I suppose that would be a waste," I reply.

"Do you really have to be up in the morning?" she asks, as though she read my mind downstairs.

"No," I admit.

"You seemed a little… reserved, like you had checked out for a bit. Are you alright?" she says. We're still stood just inside the entrance, facing each other. We can hear the rain and feel the wind buffeting us.

"Yes, yes, I'm okay. After a while I just pull away from everything. Maybe it's boredom. Like, everything becomes pointless. As if we aren't saying anything with any meaning. I don't know. Sorry, I'm rambling."

"It's okay. I think I know what you mean. It's easy to feel a bit overwhelmed with everything when you don't attach any meaning to the things going on in your life."

"That could be it," I say, leaning back against the wall, and offering Lily a smile. "Of course, that would assume there are things going on in my life," I add dourly.

"Well then, would you like to get a drink somewhere else? That would count as something 'going on' I think," Lily says, a mellifluous laugh trailing off with her last few words.

She asks this so casually yet directly too. The idea fills me with a strange sort of excitement and joy, the feeling is surprisingly intense. I nod and say yes, standing up straight. We step outside and she puts up the umbrella which I take immediately this time. She grins and puts her arm around my waist. It practically tingles. Rain is falling all around us. It has been one of those kinds of day, where it starts brightly, breaks cover, and simply persists down turning all around you to grey and the buildings look grey and the people do too. Under the umbrella, we're shielded from this.

"Where to?" Lily asks, looking up at me. I smile as her hair tickles the bottom of my chin.

Blood and Gold

Walking along Market Street always made me feel small, like an atom bustling about, at the mercy of quantum effects. Substitute quantum effects for human beings, hurrying to whatever meaningless work they did.

I was one of them too, of course.

The cold shade of Market Street, from which I had only a brief respite as I trooped around the parameter of Piccadilly Gardens, infiltrated my person like a virus. I followed the Metro Link line towards St Peter's Square. Past Burger King, Subway, Primark, Starbucks, towards Central Library and the Cenotaph. I pulled my jacket tighter around me. I knew the walk and its brightly coloured, garish sights well, culminating in solemn respectability. Grey skies above, always on the cusp of rainfall, the Rayleigh Effect in action as the clouds darkened with the density of water vapour. Again, familiar, homely even.

But today was different.

A small square shop, a few yards down a small cobbled alley, caught my eye. Books were piled up in the window just in front of dust-thickened mauve curtains. A few old gig posters were stuck to the inside of the glass. It looked like a retro bookshop, the kind that had been there forever and you'd struggle to explain how it had survived. Except I'd never seen this place. And I knew the walk well. So, who would open a retro bookshop in this economic climate, and how had it appeared so quickly?

As it happened, I was running early for work. Going in seemed like a good idea. I mean, why not?

It was only now, watching the bodies scatter and the screams ring out, watching the people trampled and the police batons swinging sabre-like, that it occurred to me that I should have carried on walking.

*

It was dark inside the shop and its only lighting was a deep red neon, the type of lighting you see in films when they want you to know the place is a bit seedy. It made me uncomfortable. The silence and emptiness augmented this sensation.

A small record stand faced the door but that aside there were three walls of books and a small counter, a rickety stool, and a doorway covered by long threads of beads. I wondered what could be back there beyond the beads, picturing jars with floating eyeballs and shrunken monkey paws, when the reality was probably stocks of books. And still… my head was telling me to leave. This was a weird place and I had somewhere to be. But I couldn't. Some compulsion drew me in deeper.

I examined the bookshelves and found an eclectic mix of authors from Hunter S. Thompson to J.G Ballard to Proust, Proulx and Arundhati Roy. Varied, but not unusual. There was no discernible order to the way the books were presented. And in amongst the well-known names were… strange looking books. Foreign languages, from French to maybe Russian and others I couldn't guess at, and then some books that were completely unmarked. The unmarked books tended to be older, worn hard backs, with creases like crow's feet. The organiser in me felt a little stab of pain and irritation at the complete anarchy that was the shop's display.

I looked around me, at the ceiling fan whirling lightly, the old horror film posters adorning the walls (*A Nightmare on Elm Street*, *Halloween*, *Friday 13th*), back to the vinyl record stand by the entrance. The place looked like the inner sanctum of a well-read teenage boy loner. Which is why, when the threads of beads rattled, denoting the entrance of the proprietor of the shop, I was surprised to see a young woman with electric blue hair and white-framed glasses, probably a similar age to me, step through them. She had the rounded cheeks of someone who smiled and laughed often.

"You look so… normal," she said, pausing, licking her top lip as if lost in thought. "I like your hair, it frames your face well," she added, stepping forward and leaning on the counter. She was wearing a purple velvet cloak over a mustard-coloured blouse. Probably from a vintage shop. No shortage of those up the road in and around Affleck's Palace.

"Um, thank you," I replied, unsure how to proceed. The silence clung on and, though it was brief, I found it to be unbearable, like being sat in the back of a taxi. "Have you been open long?" I asked.

"Yes and no."

"Right," I said, completely at a loss. I was about to turn and edge towards the door when she spoke again, stepping out from behind the counter.

"I think I have something you'd like. Here, come here. That's it, stand right there. Everyone who comes in here is looking for something, after all. I mean, why would you come in, otherwise? Now where is it? No, no, something more personal."

I could feel the expression on my face, the sheer surprise, eyes wide. And I noticed a tiny lisp in the woman's voice, which seemed to create a sibilance on the letter 's'. I stood still, precisely where she'd directed me, and she seemed to be swaying like a charmed cobra as she glanced over the titles on the shelf before her. The dark wall of books shifted out of focus, as if the books were melding with the darkness and creating an effect similar to Turner or Edvard Munch.

"Eureka!" she cried, causing me to jump. I was half caught between fascination and the desire to escape. She turned towards me, her face suddenly solemn. "This is it. Take it. It's yours," she said, shoving the book into my hands.

"Um, how much…"

"No, no, it's *yours*."

"Right. Okay."

"Are you off to work, honey? White blouse, trousers, kitten heels. Office attire. Do you enjoy it?"

"I, er, don't mind it. The pay is okay."

"You're probably worth more though, right?"

"I, um, guess so."

"I won't keep you anyway, enjoy the diary."

And with that short exchange, conducted at such close quarters I could smell her perfume (but not distinguish the brand) and hairspray, she swept back behind the counter and through to the back, beads rattling behind her.

A diary, she'd said. I looked down at the book she'd wrapped my hands around, as if passing me top secret documents down some dimly lit alley. It was unmarked.

*

The day passed without incident. I'd stuffed the diary into my bag and continued walking to work, just making it in time. But all day my head had been elsewhere, attempting to process the encounter at the bookstore. Not just how I'd never noticed the place before, but how the woman had been with me, how she'd spoken to me. When she said, 'you're probably worth more, right?', I'd been so off-kilter with the absurdity of her demeanour that I'd not been able to string a coherent thought together. Well, yes, as it happens, I am worth more. A damn sight more. Not that I've got any hope of conveying that to my bosses. They're too consumed by the goings on in their own little bubble that they don't recognise the hard work happening elsewhere in the business. If I could, I'd leave, but I can't afford to, what with the flat and other expenses. And it's not like the grass would be any greener on the other side.

But it struck me as strange, how the woman had zeroed in on that feeling, and picked it out so casually, like plucking an apple from a tree.

I made coffee and collapsed into my sofa, eyes closed for a moment. Beside the mug of coffee sat the diary. I'd yet to open it. I couldn't pinpoint the origin of my trepidation but I felt like I was mentally having to build up toward opening it. Whatever secrets lay within its pages, the woman from the bookstore had insisted they were *mine*. They were *for me* and *me alone*. Throughout the day this sentiment had taken root. I opened my eyes and opened the first page.

16 August 1819

I closed my eyes again.

The date seemed familiar to me. Why, I couldn't recall.

I opened my eyes and I was stood in a field amongst a crowd. I had to shield my eyes as the high sun glared a warning back at me. Voices were raised, and then people were scrambling. Clattering into each other. Scattering. Animal sounds, and a thunderous pounding of hooves, then the sound of pain. The bodies broke before me and hot, wet liquid sprayed across my face. A taste of iron. People were being trampled into the grass all around. The cries of death, the final cries of life. Before me, rising on its hind legs, an unknown beast, silhouetted against the angry glare of the sun. The beast towered over me like an inexorable tidal wave and collapsed its oppressive form upon me.

I awoke with a jolt and overturned the mug of coffee. Shit. I jumped up to grab the kitchen roll. Only as I stood up did I sense the utter exhaustion in my limbs and the thick sheen of sweat upon my skin. Halting abruptly, I turned to look down at my coffee table. I inhaled deeply, closed my eyes a moment, and then exhaled. The diary sat there, a ring of hot coffee surrounding it like a moat. But the book itself was bone-dry.

*

I'd overslept. Today was Saturday, so I hadn't expressly needed to be anywhere, but I hated sleeping in. I was going to go to the gym early but I felt heavy and lethargic, as if I hadn't recovered from sleeping so long, and didn't really want to go now. A waste of all that money I'm paying for membership. Sometimes it seemed all I did was waste money, work to earn more, then waste that too. I wondered if this was the curse of being single. But then, I didn't have time for a boyfriend or a girlfriend anyway, so the entire conversation was redundant.

I dragged myself out of bed and showered, then put on some coffee. I'd treated myself to one of those Bosch Tassimo coffee makers and I was now dependent on it for sustenance and vitality. I'd almost splashed out on a De'Longhi, but I'd just about resisted and bought one more my price range. The Tassimo had been a solid servant so far.

I sat in the living room with my coffee and a slice of toast and stared at the diary on the coffee table. The bone-dry diary. The diary that had somehow Force-pushed the spilled hot liquid away, leaving it settled in a neat circle around it. Yoda, this diary was not. Maybe it was Vader? I stared at it some more, expecting it to speak to me, to explain why I even owned it in the first place. I recalled the date – 16 August 1819 – and then there was that ghastly vision. I could still taste iron. Had the diary done this, had it shown me a vision? No. I was getting carried away. A few too many films and horror stories, I suspect. But now I'd slept on it, I couldn't shake the insidious feeling that something was wrong with it.

I drained my mug of coffee, finished my toast, and tidied away the pots.

I had to go back to the bookstore.

*

I'd only made it halfway up a jam-packed Market Street when I spotted an old friend of mine, Sally. She was handing out leaflets but I couldn't see what was written on them. There was a crowd of people, mostly young, all wearing red hoodies, a homogenous threatening mass, passing them out to anyone who would accept one. This kind of thing wasn't unusual along Market Street, especially on a weekend. At regular intervals there was; a man beatboxing, two young lads doing football tricks, a young girl singing, and several human statues. Although it wasn't warm out, most people were wearing jackets, it was clear and sunny, and this brought all the street performers and motivated political canvassers out to play. Sally, I suspected to be among the latter, spotted me and waved me over.

"Are you coming along tomorrow?" she asked, before I could even say 'hello'. She seemed breathlessly excited.

"To what?" I asked.

"To the protest!" she replied, her eyes ablaze. "Albert Square, outside the Town Hall, tomorrow night. We've had enough of the establishment, so we've organised a mass anti-capitalism protest."

"I didn't know there was a protest happening," I said, wondering how I'd missed it. I'd been pretty wrapped up in work of late, maybe I'd been completely zoned-out?

"Where've you been for the past week?! It's going to be huge and there's strong rumours a few major leadership figures will be in attendance. It's about human worth and how capitalism has failed. You should come along. I mean, it's the 21st century and people still read *The Wealth of Nations* like it's the freaking *Bible*," Sally added, laughing at her own joke. I laughed too, but partially as a social cue. As if I were participating in this conversation begrudgingly. I guess I was a little anxious to get to the bookstore. But at the same time I was definitely interested in hearing more. I wondered, too, the identity of the 'we' Sally said had organised the event.

"Here," she said, handing me a leaflet, "take a look. You can read more on the website and the social media pages. See, the handles are at the bottom."

"Okay, sure. I'll take a look later. I've got to get going now though…"

"No worries, see you tomorrow!" she said brightly, turning away and making a beeline for a group of elderly women walking across the road. I was happy in a way to see her bouncing away with such verve. I'd known her since secondary school and, for as long as I could remember, she'd been involved in politics. Often, I'd just let her explain things to me and let it wash over me. I guess at the time, and even now to an extent, I'd been quite politically apathetic. Perhaps it was time to change that?

I looked down at the leaflet. There was nothing fancy about it, nothing subtle or nuanced. In bold lettering, it said 'Down with Capitalism'. Beneath that were a few lines of poetry:

'Rise like Lions after slumber
In unvanquishable number –
Shake your chains to earth like dew
Which in sleep had fallen on you –
Ye are many – they are few.'

It was from a poem by Percy Shelley. I smiled. They were really going for it with the revolutionary smackdown. I just had a feeling this sort of thing, no matter how vociferous and heartfelt, had a habit of drowning. Still, I thought perhaps I'd attend anyway. It's not like it was far for me to travel and it might be interesting to see just how popular it would prove to be. After all, there's plenty of red hoodies harassing people down Market Street. They might convince a few people to go along.

I pocketed the leaflet and set off again in the direction of the bookstore.

*

A reggae band were playing loudly on the periphery of Piccadilly Gardens. Pigeons danced around them to the beat of the tin drums. I could see water bursting skyward from the fountains a little further across the expanse. Rather than gravitate towards the music, I turned right and followed the line of buildings round. I pulled my parka around me as I passed into the shade of the tall, parallel offices and banks, following the Metro Link line down towards St Peter's Square. There were a few less people milling up and down here as it was more of a connecting street between one busy area and another. I walked and I walked, waiting to see the crusty looking bookstore just inside the cobbled alley. I walked and walked until, finally, the row of high buildings opened out into St Peter's Square and cold bright sunshine met shade.

I stopped and looked back. I span around in confusion. Slowly, I walked back into the shade. The last alley splitting the row of tall buildings was cobbled. It was identical to the one I'd stepped into before walking into the bookstore. But there were just simple brick walls here. A few large dumpsters surrounded by bin bags sat further down the alley. It was cold and dark.

The bookstore had vanished.

*

I took the scenic route back to my flat, wanting to avoid an in-depth analysis of capitalism's failures from my friend and her crowd in red. It's not like I don't already know, sat here alone in my expensive studio flat wondering how I'd missed the week-long build-up to a mass event taking place around the corner from where I live.

And then there was the diary.

Sat there on the coffee table, alone but stoic, staring at me.

I stretched my arms shaking out their stiffness, then collapsed onto my two-seater settee and glanced out of the window. I could see the dark-glass metropolis of Shudehill Coach Station from my flat. People bustled about like ants in a formicarium, almost climbing on top of each other. Each person seemingly in their own little world, with their own small task to complete, and plodding on towards the task's inevitable conclusion. And then... what? Rinse and repeat? Everything looked grey. Even as I thought this, raindrops began to fall, creating little comet-like lines down the window. I enjoyed the rain. I found watching its steady downpour from the comfort of my home peaceful.

Eventually, I pulled my attention back indoors. The diary continued to watch me with the dead eyes of an apex predator. I sighed. There was nothing for it. I leant forward and picked up the diary. Automatically, I inhaled deeply, and closed my eyes.

The street was open and flanked with lines of people. Their dress was smart but... old. Like that of a period drama perhaps. Sunday best. Already I was sweating beneath my clothes, the sun close to being directly above us in the clear blue sky. Given my anachronistic dress, I found it strange nobody paid me any special attention.

I looked in the direction everyone seemed to be facing and could see an open croft. Despite a few patches of grass, it was almost entirely swamped with men, women, and children. A few people still trailed in; others were hanging around the edges. There were banners held high on wooden poles to which each segmented group gravitated around. At the far end were piles of brushwood. The croft was surrounded by brick and stone buildings with several avenues and streets trailing from it, such as the one I stood in now. Two young men on horseback, and wearing red military uniforms, trotted along the middle of the street. One of the horses pulled at its reins twitchily, its neck straining to the left. The people lining the streets seemed tense, quiet. Their eyes followed the men on horseback as they passed through.

The clip clop of horseshoes was, for several minutes, all that could be heard.

I gazed around me, allowing the scene to sink in. The clothing, the buildings, the streets, each was in some way familiar yet clearly not of my time. The diary had transported me somewhere. And, as far as I could tell, the people here couldn't see me. Part of me was afraid and wanted to run away. But another part, the greater part, felt compelled to investigate.

Although still in an uncomprehending haze, I set off walking towards the crowd, passing a woman holding a crying baby as I went.

*

As I walked closer I could see a line had been cleared through the centre of the crowd. A raised platform stood in the middle as a focal point with several people stood upon it. A group of women all wearing loose white linen dresses were by its side.

I knew now this was the location of the hustings.

I was in St Peter's Field. The year was 1819. Perhaps the diary had chosen to infect me with clarity – now it was too late to escape. Whatever power it was using, it had veiled me in confusion and darkness for some time, exercising its will over mine. I wasn't under its control; I was under its influence.

With this realisation came fear. But I still felt the same compulsion to see this through, to walk into the crowd and experience fully what I was being shown.

I entered the crowd and began to ease my way through the people. Old, young, big, small, man, woman, child, black, white. This composite crowd represented everyone, it seemed. And it did. From Rochdale to Urmston, from Wigan to Mossley, from Stockport to Royton, and everywhere in between. Dressed in the finest clothes they owned. Thousands were here, and the rest of Manchester was dead. The crowd seemed happy. I could hear music playing. Different songs coming from different directions. Each person had come here today for hope and fairness. Others had come for blood and gold.

I was among the banners now. Several metres high, they each carried a sincere slogan. A blue banner with yellow writing states, 'No more Corn Laws', and a green banner with gold writing reads, 'Liberty and Fraternity'. Most are in this vein. The people carry them in earnest. I could read the white banner of the women stood by the platform, too. It read: 'Let us die like men and not be sold like slaves'.

As I pushed further in, though, a few complaints could be heard. The manner of speaking was a little odd to my ears, but the complaints seemed to be about the heat and fatigue. There were flushed faces and men and women mopping brows with handkerchiefs around me. The bodies exacerbated the heat and I could feel my legs going weak. But still, I pushed onwards until I was close enough to see the platform clearly. The men who'd formed a channel between the crowd were all uniformed and stood like soldiers in a regiment, upright and formal. Through that channel a carriage rolled along. Its heavy wheels indenting the grass beneath it trampling the multitude of blades. Around me, the crowd edged forward in unison, expectation, hope. The music had stopped.

And then the screams began.

The crowd surged forwards and people fell. I only just managed to stay on my feet but heard squeals of pain nearby. And then I saw them coming. A cavalry charge; each of the riders in blue jackets and full military attire. Ineffective, but battling through the swathes of people who were now rushing to get away. Some of the horses had become stuck and any sense of formation was lost. And all of this was happening right before my eyes.

As people ran, others fell, and were trampled underfoot. Knocked unconscious, bloodied, the people were being brutalised within a whirlwind of confusion and aggression. The grass churned like a river of blood beneath flailing hoofs and desperate feet. Banners were trampled into the mud.

And then the glint of steel under the bright afternoon sun.

Flashing down from great heights, the cavalry soldiers had drawn their sabres and were slashing away at anyone or anything in reach. The horses were panicking too. Kicking out, jerking their heads this way and that like in the throes of a seizure. They were breaking bones and splicing flesh under the peaceful afternoon sun.

It came from nowhere.

To my right, bursting through the crowd. A man stood before me felt the full force of the soldier's sabre. His blood splattered across my face. The taste of iron. Within this world of screaming and pain, I heard the thunderous hooves bearing down upon me. I saw the sun disappear behind a towering beast. I felt the crushing weight of death.

*

I opened my eyes and the ceiling of my flat, with a simple light-fitting in the centre, stared back at me. An immediate spasm of pain shot through my back. I raised my head slightly and saw the splayed, splintered limbs of my little coffee table. I grabbed the settee with my right hand and began to pull myself up. I'd be bruised, no doubt, but I seemed to have fortuitously avoided any serious damage or open wounds. It hadn't been an immensely sturdy coffee table, though quite how I'd crashed through it and no one had come to check on me, with the walls being quite thin in my building, was anyone's guess.

I looked down at the splintered wreckage and saw, beneath it all, the diary. Unmarked and stolid. I had a sense that if I set fire to it, the flames would merely fizzle out or be swallowed whole by a gaping papery mouth. Outside I could see was dark. How long had I been out for? I checked my watch, but it read 13:00 so I took the hint it was broken. It was cheap anyway, so I couldn't expect much from it. My phone was in my bedroom. I'd check the time and go to bed. On my way, I grabbed some painkillers from the cabinet in the bathroom.

*

I woke with a start in the night, draped in sweat. It wasn't an especially warm night, nor did I recall dreaming anything frightening. I swung myself out of bed, forgetting my sore back for a split second, and winced. When the aching had subsided, I rose and headed to the kitchen area for a glass of water – I suddenly found I was parched.

The tiles surrounding the kitchen top sent cold snaps through the soles of my feet. I ran the tap and filled a glass before gulping it down. Moonlight shone through the window, a sensual illumination upon my living room. And there, impossibly, on my unbroken coffee table, sat the diary.

My cold feet slowly edged towards it. I reached out one hand, the moonlight softly caressing my thin fingers, and wrapped them around the diary.

I remained where I was, in my flat, back aching, holding a dog-eared diary. I exhaled. I flicked the light switch and blinked a few times as my eyes adjusted to the light. I sat down and opened the diary at the back page.

17 August 1819

The day following the Peterloo Massacre. The last entry into this diary was written the day after the disaster. I read on.

Yesterday, my world ended.
The horse and rider did not stop. They sought no audience with me after the event. The horse collided with me and William, poor, tiny William, was thrown from my arms. I watched the horses gallop away. William did not move again.
Yesterday, my world ended.

Beneath this, there seemed to be a name. The first name was smudged slightly, as if water had dripped upon it. The second name was 'Fildes'.

I did not know the name.

I closed the diary and placed it back on the impossible coffee table. Whoever wrote this had lost a child during the carnage. I thought back to the two riders on horseback who had trotted past me. There was a woman holding a small child too. Could this diarist be the same woman I had passed when walking towards the gathering in the croft? That small child had probably died within an hour of our passing each other.

Blood and gold. Paid in blood and gold.

I stood up and flicked the lights off.

The injustice of it all. I got back in bed, pulled the covers back around me, and wept. Eventually, exhausted, I fell asleep.

*

I slept in again and, today, Sunday, I felt no guilt. I wasn't irritated, I simply felt rested. I used the good old Bosch Tassimo and felt strangely grateful to it for providing me with good coffee for as long as it had. It had served me well. On the kitchen top, I noticed the leaflet Sally had given me.

The anti-capitalist protest was today.

I felt a strong urge to attend.

I thought briefly about taking a slight detour to see whether the bookstore had reappeared. But something told me not to bother. Call it an instinct.

*

The protest was officially due to start at half past seven. A platform would be erected in the centre of Albert Square, right under the nose of the Town Hall, the epitome of establishment, and several prominent left-wing figures would be giving speeches. I'd finally taken the time to look up the event on social media and was a little surprised to see just how much traction it had gained. Given this, I thought I'd walk down a little early and arrive for seven-ish, knowing there was a chance there'd be a decent crowd.

I turned along Princess Street before I reached St Peter's Square, not wishing to see that little cobble-stoned alley, and whether a grimy, retro bookstore was open there. I sensed something big was happening when I heard the loud hum of voices and music booming from what sounded to be powerful stereo speakers. Car horns beeped too, the music of the modern city. Walking towards me, away from these sounds, was a woman cradling a small child in her arms. As our paths crossed our eyes met and she smiled at me. And then she was gone. I continued walking, wondering what I would find as I turned the corner.

I was unprepared for what greeted me.

I walked out into Albert Square, the Town Hall to my left. There must have been thousands of people. It was crammed with people. Men, women, children. Food stands were serving long queues dotted about the edges. Others were selling magazines or scarves or bits of tat that might well have been badges or buttons. The darkness of evening had settled in and the streetlamps were alight. Fairy lights decorated the trees standing firm and strong in the square. A full moon adorned the sky like the brightly lit star atop a Christmas tree. The excitement of the crowd was palpable.

I walked along the path, tracing the line of road running south-west, until I was outside the entrance to the Town Hall. Two policeman riding enormous police horses were casually approaching. I froze. In that moment, for a split-second, all sounds were silenced, but for the clip-clop of the horses' hoofs on the stone slabs of the road.

I inhaled deeply. And I was back. The festival atmosphere engulfed me once again. I looked around, at the towering buildings surrounding the square, at the neo-classical architecture of the Town Hall behind me. And then back at the crowd. Under the combined light of the streetlamps and the moon the faces of the thronging crowd were like a shimmering lake. Within these deep waters I caught a flash of blue. Blinking, I focused on the blue. Just across the street, stood facing me, looking straight at me, was a woman in a flowing ankle-length jacket, with blue hair, round, happy cheeks, and white thick-rimmed glasses. She was smiling at me. And then, as if being swallowed by the shimmering depths, she turned into the crowd and disappeared.

I could see the signs being held by the crowd. 'Women's rights are Trans rights', 'Free Palestine', 'We need a universal living wage' – a collection of slogans without any consistent thread beyond that of combating oppression. And the arbiter of that oppression, the thousands present knew, was capitalism. In amongst this sea of signs I saw another that caught my eye. It read: 'Blood and Gold'.

I crossed the road in a hurry, hoping to catch the woman from the disappearing bookstore. Somehow, it seemed she'd set me on a path which led here. All because of a diary from 1819. I pushed my way into the crowd and manoeuvred through it, past the people waving their signs in earnest, past those excitedly chattering with each other about politics, a broad mixture of faces. All of them were here because they held out hope for a fairer world. I was closing in on the centre of the crowd by my best estimation. A group of women dressed in white were shouting ahead of me. I saw Sally and she smiled and waved at me, rushing towards me in her excited manner.

And then the screams began.

The Clinical Trial

I'd seen the advertisement for the trial on a holographic billboard. They're trialling the holographic technology across the city now. It will save money, they say, being able to remotely alter the ads from a centralised system.

The irony being my job is to manually replace billboard advertisements. I'd take the roll of blue-backed 120msg paper, heavier and sturdier you see, and roll it onto the hoarding. You had to stir the paste mix yourself, and safely use scaffolding and ladders, but it was an easy job. Go to the site, remove the previous poster, paste on the new one, job done. Onto the next one.

But I had no idea how to run these holographic systems. Once they were built and installed, they only needed maintaining. No paste, no scaffolding, no mixing. An art form, I used to say. Things looked bleak when they brought in the televisual ones. Holographic boards are the business though.

The short story? I'm out of a job.

Then, like I say, I saw the ad for the trial. It paid well, and it paid quickly. Maybe I sound a little casual about my predicament. Truth is, I was a couple of months' rent away from being flat broke. Desperate for anything, I signed on. Within a week, I'd been accepted.

*

The building was modern and impressive, a glass giant. Windows gleaming as blue as the clear sky above. I could see the reception and the receptionist straight ahead as I entered through the electronic revolving door. Even doors weren't manual anymore. Soon, I'll forget how to open doors.

"I'm here for the trial," I said as I reached the desk. The man behind the desk was expertly groomed with a toothpaste ad smile.

"Which trial is that, sir? We have several on."

"Oh, sorry, one moment." I fished my phone from my pocket and, using my index finger, prodded it until I found the email I'd received. "This one. Trial... Q17." I looked uneasily at the receptionist, hoping I'd come to the right place.

"Ah yes, of course, sir. Please sign in using the touchscreen to your right. I'll call the Clinical Lead to come and fetch you."

He gestured with an open palm toward the screen and then picked up the phone. I faffed about with the screen for a minute while he spoke to someone. Then he asked me to take a seat. I guess at least the art of sitting isn't something which can be replaced anytime soon. I pictured a future of disembodied balls of light floating about, human beings who'd ascended into electric godhood. The human form obsolete.

A moment later a young woman in a dark skirt, white blouse, and white lab jacket, greeted me with another toothpaste ad smile and invited me to follow her into the glass elevator.

*

I'd expected to feel an exhilaration of fear as the glass elevator shot up the centre of the glass giant.

But the elevator took us down. Into a metallic bunker of a laboratory. Endless rooms, like if Noah had built a space ark.

I was directed down several identical corridors by the young researcher, whose name was Mitsuke. I'd told her it was a beautiful name and she'd smiled.

She led me through a door into a small plain square room. In the middle of the room was a chair, placed before a large square machine. It was a hybrid of telescope, hi-tech stereo, and submarine periscope in shape. Its black metal, with honed corrugated ridges along each side, gave it a dense presence in the room. It reminded me of Kafka's *Metamorphosis*, with the giant bug in the bedroom. I couldn't take my eyes off it. Finally, I turned back to Mitsuke, who smiled knowingly and encouragingly.

"Most people view Q17 in much the same way. First, horror. Then, curiosity. Please, take a seat," she said, gesturing with an open palm.

I did as Mitsuke said, sitting down on the cold seat, and faced forwards. The indent on this side of Q17 was clearly defined to accept a human face, complete with small glass circles for the eyes to see through. They must lead to the machine's dark heart.

"The idea of Q17 is to synthesise your soul with that of a machine," Mitsuke said. Her voice seemed suddenly cold, as if she were reading from a teleprompter. "In the trial stage, we are seeking to confirm the quality and longevity of its primary functionality. First, we will engage

Q17 and synthesise your soul with the machine. We will then monitor both your body and soul. The primary aim of the Q17 project is to merge machine-based efficiency with human rationality. Do you accept the terms initially agreed upon signing?"

"Yes, I accept."

"Please place your face within the grooves and ensure your eyes are level with the glass circles."

I did as Mitsuke asked and felt the cold metal on my cheeks and forehead and lips.

"Please place your hands on the handles."

I did as Mitsuke asked.

"We will now engage Q17."

There was a rush of excruciating pain, as if my body had been slammed against a wall. And then silence.

*

I tried to reach out and touch… anything. But there was no hand to touch with. I tried to speak, to yell, to scream, to cry. But there were no instruments to do so with. There was a bright light. I was a bright light. I felt that intrinsically. But there was no physical body, only the festering sensation of potentiality. I sensed a lexicological shift. My speech patterns fading… no, evolving. Becoming more efficient. There was pain. No body to feel the pain. An overwhelming concept of pain. Who was I?

*

Mitsuke observed Q17 for several days and noted no observable physical symptoms, no shift in pulse, heart rate, and so forth.

Three days later, she reported the 100% success of the clinical trial. Each participant had merged wholly with the machine. Regrettably, detachment was unachievable and… undesirable.

Night of the Living Derek

The Hurricane jets swept through the sky above in formation, casting ripples through the spacetime continuum. At least, that's what Charlie thought. It used to be he'd run inside, when he was a little younger, hands protecting his ears, tears rushing from his eyes. He chuckled at the thought while watching the Hurricanes rattle past at enormous speeds. Little Melling Village, with its post office, one local pub, rows of bungalows, and its sprawling RAF airfield. Stood in his nana's front garden, having closed the gate behind him, he turned and walked up the path to the house. Bees buzzed about the flowers flanking the concrete road between the two gardens.

"Eee, what a racket. Now then, Charlie," his nana said, addressing him from the doorway. She looked a little smaller than the last time he'd seen her, but her face still glowed. Light green cardigan, long grey skirt, cream-coloured blouse, slippers, the Nana's Uniform. Leaning forward ever-so-slightly more than last time because her back was getting worse. Charlie noticed all these little things.

"Now then, nana," Charlie said, kissing her on the cheek. 'Now then' had always been something his grandad used to say to him, and for years, being a suburban townie, was something he hadn't a clue how to respond to. Eventually, he just came to repeat it back. His grandad wasn't here anymore, though.

"New car, is it? Was the journey okay?" his nana asked, wandering through to the quaint living room littered with photographs of children on wedding days, grandchildren, heck, even great grandchildren. Photos of grandchildren on graduation days, including Charlie's, photos of old pets. Ancient photos in black and white, grainy, mysterious. Old friends, lost friends. The living room was a treasure trove of memories. His nana walked straight through to the kitchen and flicked the kettle on.

"The journey was fine, nana, traffic was okay," Charlie answered. He let the car question slide. It was the same car as last time, and the time before that, too. "The jets are out again," he added, shouting through as he dropped his bag in the front bedroom. Hands down, the comfiest bed he'd ever slept in; he always joked it was half the reason he kept visiting. And fish and chip night, too, of course. This was the added advantage of arriving on a Friday.

"You'd think I'd get used to them, but they're just a nuisance. Your grandad used to enjoy wandering up to the airfield to watch them take off. Or from round back of The Oak," she said, settling a cup of tea onto a coaster on the coffee table. The Oak was the local pub, a place that, somehow, hadn't changed one iota as far as Charlie could remember. And that was how the locals liked it. Conveniently, it was a thirty second walk from the front door.

"I remember," Charlie said, smiling, thinking of when he'd walk down with his grandad to watch in awe. This, of course, was when he was a little older and had grown out of his run-off-with-hands-on-ears stage. The jets racing along, a torrent of precise mechanical engineering, like a man-made shark, streaming off into the great big blue above. A strange contrast with everything else in sight: the oak trees flanking the caravan park behind the pub; the birds' nests and the twittering sounds they emit; the thousands of pinecones littering the field's boundary.

Charlie always enjoyed coming to visit. When he could, he took the rare opportunity, over the weekend, in between work, to visit his nana. Although she would never admit it, she was a little lonely here.

Together, they sat and watched the quizzes on the telly, and then Charlie's uncle appeared to go and do the shopping. They'd be back with the fish and chips in a couple of hours and Charlie had organised to meet his cousin in The Oak for a couple of drinks. A nice evening was settling in and he hadn't seen him for a while, so it seemed a good chance to catch up. Charlie waved his nana and uncle off, then made the hundred-yard stroll up to the pub.

Meanwhile, elsewhere, after what felt like an eternity, a hand burst up through the earth and into the light.

*

It was the type of establishment where nothing more was required other than a simple nod and either, 'lager', or 'bitter'. A swift utterance and, as if by magic, a beer would appear before you. Sat outside on standard pub picnic benches, the fading sun on his back, Charlie was nodding along as his cousin regaled him with stories of his new house, what work needed doing to it, the amateur jobs someone had done previously, the usual type of thing that a tradesman seemed capable of spotting in a heartbeat but Charlie, being an office monkey, knew nothing about.

Being sat outside took Charlie back. Of course, it used to be a small bottle of Coca Cola rather than a beer, but the soothing sensation was similar. As time passed his grandad would let him have a sip of beer. Charlie always forgot how he'd disliked the taste the previous time and looked forward to each fresh opportunity to try it. Year by year, he'd coaxed his taste buds into obedience until, finally, he enjoyed it. Oddly, this gradual indoctrination of taste remained a warm-coated memory to Charlie.

The sign for The Oak, with a simple sketching of a tree on it, rattled above them in the light surges of breeze. Hanging baskets bursting with colour either side of the heavy green doors of the entrance. Whitewashed walls and black painted beams, thatched roof, picture perfect. Charlie had slipped into reverie. Often, it's the minor details which recall the bigger picture. Retrieving Charlie from his inner musings, his cousin recommenced speaking.

"Something right weird happened the other day, though," he said, in a Yorkshire accent as broad as his shoulders, which is to say exceedingly broad.

"Go on," Charlie said, before taking a swig of his drink.

"Well," he began, "I was out back at me mam and dads' place, and I heard the jets going over, as usual. And then the noise just… stopped. I mean, I hadn't seen the plane but, I know the sound, you know? There was at least more than one and they just seemed to vanish. Like they'd disappeared through a wormhole or something."

Charlie gave it some thought. Logically, what his cousin was telling him was impossible, therefore there had to be an explanation. Perhaps it had been something else, a noise that was a close enough imitation that it latched onto his cousin's expectations when he heard it. Instead of wondering what the noise was, he assumed it was the jets going over. Perhaps it was a neighbour with a grumpy hedge-trimmer? But Charlie didn't want to undermine his cousin. He seemed certain about the truncated trail of sound's origins, and equally certain of its unusual and abrupt absence. So Charlie simply agreed it was unusual, and went back to drinking his drink.

Charlie wasn't to know that his cousin's bizarre wormhole theory was closer to the mark. It was, however, less quantum physics and more Bermuda Triangle as the planes found themselves slipping through a barrier which hadn't, seconds prior, existed.

The two cousins sat in silence for a minute or two, draining the glasses before them.

It was about this time, as Charlie wandered inside to replace their empty receptacles, that a series of hands punched through the lightly-patted-down earth and grasped at fresh air.

*

As Charlie returned to the table out front with two spume-topped pints, his cousin was finishing a phone-call.

"That was uncle Tim," he said, "apparently, they're stuck in traffic, and loads of it. Thinks there's roadblocks, but no idea why. You might have to wait for fish and chips!"

Charlie groaned. If he stayed out longer with his cousin, he knew how cloudy eyed he'd be returning to the bungalow. But there was nothing to be done. At least he wasn't on his own. He gazed across the road at the row of terraced houses (the few two-storey buildings on this main stretch of road), neat and tidy, matching brown-brick, matching brown window frames. A white cat lounged upon a wall. Nothing unusual in that. Black cats were the bad omens, after all. The cat turned to look at him, disdain writ upon its squashed face.

"It's good of you to come, like," said his cousin, his tone meeker, guilt-ridden. "I know we only live round the corner really, but we've been so busy with the house, and work's really taken off…"

"Life has a habit of getting in the way," Charlie responded, seeing his cousin struggling to find the right words. And it wasn't like Charlie didn't feel a weight of guilt that he couldn't visit more often. The loss of their grandad hung as a spectre over not just the family but the whole community, especially in such a small village where everyone knew everyone. When he'd died it had been like ripping out the keystone of a bridge and seeing the remains struggle to stay together. They'd recovered, over time. Not by replacing the keystone, but by building a new bridge.

"Well, yeah, basically," his cousin said, "you're always the one who knows what to say."

They quietly touched glasses and drank deeply.

A moment passed before his cousin stood and went inside to refill their glasses. The last two had slid down their throats with the smoothness of honey.

As Charlie sat outside waiting for his cousin, he noticed something unusual about the sky. Everything was still. Suspended in the air. As if everything had just… stopped. And it had stopped. While they'd continued with their evening, and time passed, a strange barrier had risen around the village, preventing anything from coming in, or going out. Odd ripples in the fabric of space and time had caused a disturbance in reality. Little Melling Village was now hidden from the rest of the world, separate, or, perhaps more accurately, forgotten.

Charlie's cousin stepped out holding two more drinks and placed them on the table. As he looked up, he let out an inadvertent groan, a noise of surprise. He tapped Charlie on the shoulder, raised his arm, and pointed. Charlie followed the invisible line springing forth from said finger.

Walking along the road, past the long row of hedges, past the bungalows, were a host of figures, silhouetted, because night had drawn in like a translucent veil across the village. There were, perhaps, ten or so of them. As they walked along, not quickly, not slowly, silence seemed to fall. To be more exact, it was as if all sound around them was being swallowed up by their very presence. And in the air, a fetid quality, floating towards The Oak. As the figures reached the circle of light emitted by The Oak's outdoor lamps, Charlie, his cousin, and the few others sat outside, recoiled. Covered in dirt, one noticeably brushing a worm from his jacket, these people looked like they'd been dragged there through a freshly ploughed field. Their flesh labile, discoloured. To Charlie, the new arrivals appeared ferocious, eyeing each one of the innocent and inebriated locals sat on the benches outside The Oak.

Silence. The crowd of men and women, all dressed smartly, over-dressed for a Friday at The Oak, stopped just within the circle of light. It seemed to stop them momentarily, as if shuddering at the sudden brightness.

The sign for The Oak rattled above them, a susurration of chains and heavy wood in the wind. What was actually happening was, in fact, an unchaining, the release of bonds to the afterlife, if only for an evening. People who were mere memories were here in actuality, and they'd fallen back into their own memories, returning to the place they would always go on a Friday evening, their regular haunt.

One man stepped forward. Only now was it clear how grey and mottled his skin was, and how stained and dark his eyes were, like black marbles.

"We haven't missed last orders, have we?"

*

Annette, the landlord for as long as anyone could remember, which said more about her denizens' memories than the length of time she'd had The Oak, served everyone without stuttering. A remarkable achievement considering she'd attended about half of the funerals and worked all of the wakes.

The new customers, undead one and all, spilled out into the front, where several tables were empty, and carried on as if nothing untoward or mysterious were taking place. An odour followed the crowd. Not entirely unpleasant, a mixture of earthy goodness and an array of perfumes added during embalming, with just a hint of putrefaction beneath this heady cover. Charlie and his cousin sat where they'd been sat all night, sipping their beers, communicating through facial expressions and eyebrow lifts. Above them, a full moon poked above a cloud like a nosy neighbour.

"I know you two," declared a voice. A creaking voice,

like a door in need of oiling. A man edged over, drink in grey hand. Quite how he knew Charlie and his cousin, they did not know, because one of the man's eye sockets was empty, and the other glazed over with something the texture of egg white. Without any ceremony he sat down beside them and looked them up and down, as if assessing the structure of their bodies for any sign of wear and tear or risks and hazards. "Aye, I know you two. Jim's grandsons. You're a lot bigger now. Especially you, champ, crikey, you're bigger than your uncle Tim!" he exclaimed with such effusive warmth that Charlie and his cousin couldn't help but smile. This strange evening seemed to be taking yet another strange turn.

"How did you know our grandad?" asked Charlie, leaning forward, blinking away a few of the beer swirls.

"We were brickies together, back in the day. Both retired round here, so we'd come down here on occasion, throw a few quoits, that kind of thing. Not that Jim ever really retired, eh? I'm sure he was only meant to potter around that big garden twice a week, but you couldn't keep him away! I remember him saying Sal would get on his case about resting once in a while, but you know what he were like, belligerent until the end. How's Sal keeping?" said the undead man who, now he'd discovered he could speak in the land of the living once more, seemed unable to stop.

It took Charlie and his cousin a second or two to click that he was referring to their nana. Charlie's cousin answered. "She's good, aye. A bit lonely, you know, what with grandad being gone and us all being busy, life getting in the way, you know? But Charlie's here for the weekend, drives up when he can."

Charlie nodded and, he thought, the undead man

attempted to wink at him, assumedly in approval but it really was hard to tell.

"Good lad," said the undead man, "not sure if you remember me too well, but I'm Derek. We had the old boxer, Tully, if you remember the old boy?" he added hopefully.

"Oh yeah," Charlie exclaimed, "I do! I was never too keen on dogs, but Tully was the exception. Nicest dog I ever met. Grandad would always stop when we walked past your house and wait for Tully to amble over so we could pet him. We'd walk down to the River Spool and play pooh sticks, me and my sisters too. I'd forgotten about that…"

"It's funny what you forget in time, eh?" Derek said, pouring the remainder of his drink down his throat. The skin was so thin you could almost see the amber liquid gushing down. "I'm surprised Jim isn't here, to be honest. This seems right up his street this kind of venture."

Charlie and his cousin laughed the guilty laugh of those who thought something a little dark in unison and couldn't quite contain themselves.

"He'd have had a hard time," Charlie's cousin said, "he were cremated!"

The three of them fell about laughing before breathing in and exhaling the deep sigh which follows a bout of laughter, the laughter's last calls. In their joy, they'd forgotten entirely they were in the company of someone who'd passed to the other side several years prior. Charlie and his cousin were lost in the thrall of discussing their grandad, and Derek was lost in the thrall of life. Life lost, life lived.

Across the road, the white cat stretched out its front limbs, paws out, and yawned. Its desultory interest in the adjacent commotion was waning, as is a cat's prerogative.

As quickly as they'd appeared, the undead crowd began drinking up and gesticulating it was time to leave. At that, Derek stood up too.

"Stay for another," Charlie said, looking into the murky white of one eye and the empty socket of the other.

"Sorry lads, can't. Barrier's going down soon. Whatever it is that aligns to allow this, it's about to un-align. Unless you want to be brushing away a pile of Derek dust in an hour or so, we'd better shift. It's been a pleasure. If I bump into Jim I'll be sure to say you said hello." And with that he nodded goodbye and joined the departing group. Up the road they walked, fading into silhouette and, eventually, fading from view.

*

Silence.

As if all sound had gone with the party of undead.

And then breathing.

Slowly, gradually, life returned to The Oak and, one by one, the regulars slipped out the wide, green front doors and, with a brief nod or mumbled goodbye, slunk off home. Just like any normal Friday night. Charlie looked up to see a slender cloud drifting across the full moon – everything in the heavens was moving as it should. And across the road a white cat purred, the way a dog might bark at the moon, before leaping from its perch and disappearing through a cat-flap and into its home, no doubt in search of food.

Charlie and his cousin stood and stretched their limbs, his cousin's arms seeming interchangeable with the powerful wide wings of an albatross. As they stood a car drove past and beeped at them, causing them to jump. Uncle Tim and their nana had returned. Charlie and his cousin looked at each other and an unspoken pact to never speak of what transpired tonight was agreed. The evening now seemed to have flashed by as quickly as a Hurricane jet. They shook hands and set off in separate directions.

*

Bustling about the kitchen putting things away, Charlie's nana was grumbling about the traffic.

"Never known anything like it," she muttered.

"Fish and chips at this hour."

"I'll get plates under the oven."

As she pattered about like a small, grey Tasmanian Devil, leaving ordered chaos in her wake, Charlie sat down with a pint of water in the living room, gazing around at the photographs, the memories. His head was clearing. And his stomach growling. Fish and chips at this hour sounded perfect.

"Thanks nana," he shouted through, interrupting her tirade of complaints.

"You're welcome, love," she shouted back, returning to her bustling.

And so they sat, and they ate, and watched a little television, and then they went to bed. Charlie felt like he'd returned to one of the comfortable memories of his youth, and, with that, he drifted off to sleep in the comfiest bed he'd ever known.

Defiance

It was what brought us here, I guess. The search for more. For more what, you say? Well, I wouldn't know about that. I'm just trying to survive.

It's cold in here, and wet, dark, dank, and filthy. Things crawl about in the corners. Cockroaches really can survive anywhere. For the past week or so this has been home, for me and the lads. And the lass, of course. I can't tell you much about this place, or the year, or the time. The truth is, I'm not sure those things even exist anymore. Sometimes I wonder if we even exist anymore. It's been a long campaign. I suppose I can start with what I do know. What I do know is that sat in this circle around our feeble and failing heat lamp is a collection of people who know about as much as I do. That is, going clockwise; Jimmy, Scraps, Tomboy, Jin, and, back round to me, Carter. What else do I know? We're all armed, standard laser-sight beam rifles. We're all carrying standard kit in our belts, mini-medical kit, food capsules, standard issue knife, the usual. Tomboy isn't too happy with the new threads though, faded red camo with dark stripes. But hey, you've got to adapt. She did smile when I said the red brings out the bloodlust in her eyes.

So that's the gang. We're stranded for now and it

doesn't look like we're getting out of here any time soon. We've not heard a peep. There never was anything good on the radio.

"Carter, were you there at Moon Rising?" asks Jimmy. His voice sounds like it's been through a sawmill. His hands are mimicking rolling a cigarette again. I'm not sure he notices he's doing it. I wouldn't mind a cigarette myself, but these fibreglass helmets are hardly convenient for it. And Jimmy, well, he's a bit retro, doesn't go in for those refillable vapour things, sticks to the proper tobacco, the stuff that'll kill you. Says everything will in the end, might as well pick your poison. I can never think of an argument back.

"Sure Jimmy, I was there, with 7th Company, got stranded then too." Tomboy and Scraps are watching us quietly; they were too young for Moon Rising. They're lucky.

"Surrounded by Japanese we were, like one of those old legends people tell about a place called Vietnam, where the enemy appear like ghosts from the jungle and you don't know who you're shooting at or what's real and what's not anymore. Just like that, I tell you, freaking terrifying. Glad we saw them off. Never did like them anyway."

"You shouldn't be glad about death," scolded Tomboy, "it's ugly."

"Eh?" Jimmy is confused. "Why not?"

I can see it's just ignorance. Ignorance has worn down everything. It's like we've evolved, stagnated, and devolved all in the same time-span, each of these things running naked, adjacent to each other, laughing. Idealists think they can change people's ideas, but you need more than fancy sounding theories. That's not enough for proper change, proper change needs a different attitude and the human attitude will forever suffer from amnesia and greed and stupidity. All three of those things are why we're here in the first place.

"Anyway, what was I saying? Yeah, Carter, you probably heard we captured one of their elite, was supposed to be masterminding that entire eastern campaign. He couldn't even watch his own arse. They put him in front of a firing squad and asked him if he had any last words, you know what he said?"

"Wait," says Jin, "you took his life?"

"Well, not me, personally. Don't look so offended Jin, he was the enemy. War is black and white, there's them and there's us," said Jimmy. Now Jimmy's stood up and pulled his knife out. He can be pretty animated when he's in story mode. "When I'm in battle, it don't matter what happens so long as I come out alive. They take this. And they take that. I get out," he adds, thrusting his knife at invisible foes, twisting the final one. He retreats to his bunk and sits down, staring at the ground. Sometimes he just needs a minute to himself.

Jin is sitting quiet in the corner. If I needed to describe him in a single word, 'quiet' would suffice. Or, maybe a better fit would be 'contemplative'. I heard a rumour he was a reformed Buddhist monk. I think I replied along the lines of 'how can a monk who is no longer a monk be reformed?', but gossiping soldiers aren't renowned for their profound understanding of semantics or ancient eastern religions. His head suited its current buzz-cut better than it would being shaved, but I doubt that was the reasoning behind any 'reformation'. He's intelligent and placid, which always makes me wonder what drove him to sign up. There had been a lot of violence in his native Tibet over time, mostly with neighbouring China, always talking boundaries. It was all so… human. Whatever led him here, I was thankful for. If that happened to be something tragic, well, I'd reconciled myself with that some time ago too. Currently, he had a small book in his hands: ancient poetry.

I suppose we all could have done with something to do. Like I say, we've been here a week already and it feels much longer. Frankly, I say a week, but it could be two days, it could be a month. I'm glad we can't taste the air; I can practically see the spores. Soon, we'll forget there's an outside at all and start scratching hellish mangled faces into the walls like the first humans all that time ago.

The last place I knew where we were… the skirmish by the sea, I guess. I say skirmish because it was over quickly, not because it was lightweight. When they started this war I think they massively underestimated what we were up against out here. And when I say they, I mean the guys back in Washington and Beijing, sat behind bulletproof rumours of supposed mass weaponry being developed underground. Someone told me governments had used this excuse before, but I wouldn't know about that. He'd said it was an age ago anyway. I just hope that some way, somehow, this all gets back to them and they see the hell they've put us through in the name of nothing. Maybe the big wigs will take consolation in being right. These guys have developed weapons. Stuff so sophisticated we might as well be pointing our fingers at them and shouting 'piouw, piouw'. Back at the sea, they emerged from underground, right through the arid surface. There came a tremor first, and the dusky water shivered under a starless sky. Then they came, these great mechanical monsters driving straight up through the ground like dolphins effortlessly breaking the ocean surface; red dust scattered everywhere like fog, blinding us. The assembled companies ran in all directions. It felt like gunfire surrounded us and a scarlet storm raged. The dust settled and those gangly, lolloping, heavily armed mutants emerged from their machines. It was an ambush. Most of our lot ran straight into their legion emerging from the red dunes. We had our backs to the sea. We were trapped.

Tomboy kicked an empty tin across the cave and collapsed onto her bunk. She'd taken to pacing up and down once in a while.

"I hate killing time," she said.

"Patience, Tomboy," replied Jin, "time will always pass, you will only pass once."

I could see she didn't know what to make of this and so she went quiet. Scraps sidled over to her, sat beside her on her bunk, but didn't say a word. He hadn't said a word in all the time I'd known him. He was from a remote part of Eastern Africa, one ravaged by an internal war a long time ago, I'm not sure how long. Most of northern Africa is run by various rebel militia, peddling guns, drugs and people. It's a shame. There's not much left of the old continent, at least not until you hit the deep south – the old powers deserted the continent as soon as was convenient. No surprise there.

When Scraps was young, his tongue had been cut out for misbehaving, or so they say. Who they are and where they heard that, I don't know. It's a sad story. He's a nice kid, and very loyal, particularly to Tomboy. There's a bit of an intensity between them, I'm not sure it's romantic but it's somehow profound. When you've been in the forces as long as I have you start to get a good feel for the bonds between people. Unless you're Jimmy and you can't see beyond what's straight in front of you. He's basically a train. He is, however, useful in a fight. I think we've got him to thank for making it this far. Back by the sea it was bleak, enemy forces closed in. I remember being startled for a separate reason: they didn't need a suit to breathe; they'd adapted. Another sign we were in over our heads.

The five of us broke away toward the sparse flatland. If we could make it across that before someone tailed us we'd reach the rocky terrain that rose in the distance and find cover. Screams and wails splintered the consistent beam-fire, a wall of noise in which any man or woman could get lost and remember what it's like to be a little child in a big world. To our right they came, a small group of them from behind a dune. Time stood still and I looked round at Tomboy and Scraps. Jin pushed his way in front of them, but I was frozen. That moment of hesitation is all it takes. I guess it can happen to anyone. But not Jimmy. He charged head on, yelling as he went like some berserker, high on hallucinogenic shit, into the flames. Jimmy was always a good marksman but this was something else. Shot after shot hitting its mark; each duck and weave seeing theirs miss by millimetres. Jin weighed in after that, and then the rest of us, firing as we ran. And soon the fighting was behind us, a distant nightmare.

Tomboy and Scraps remained huddled together on her bunk, Tomboy muttering a line to him once in a while. She was a funny one. Disowned by her religious zealot parents for being gay, ostracised by the broadly masculine forces for being a woman, aggressive and proud. All the attitudes of the past that weren't back there where they belong. Doesn't time make everything better? Ha.

Tomboy had it rough but she comes across as gritty and tough. Then you see her with Scraps and I remember that she's just a kid, scared and alone out here. The fear never subsides, or the loneliness, you just develop coping mechanisms. Most turn to drink. Some turn to God. Me? I turn to memories, mostly of family, and convince myself I'm trying to preserve things the way they were. It's been a long time on the road now and a lot has probably changed. I remember things the way they were and will keep on seeing them that way. I think that's why I'm running it all through my head, so it's all preserved *somewhere*.

"Scraps is cold," said Tomboy, "it's like home, he says. Reminds him of the night time."

"How could he say all that?" asked Jimmy curtly.

"He says things in ways you wouldn't understand," she snapped back.

Coldness ran through the air. Sharp, incisive, like a scalpel.

Ordinarily, I'd have expected Jimmy to take that quick retort as an affront. I'd already risen from my haunches, ready to put myself between them. But he just nodded and let it go. I could even see surprise on the faces of Tomboy and Scraps. Jin remained calm. The man could be bleeding out from a wound and he'd still be unperturbed.

"I don't understand much…" Jimmy began, as if stirring from a deep sleep. "I don't understand much…" and he trailed off again.

No, Jimmy. Neither do I. None of us understand why this is happening.

*

We'd turned the heat lamp off for a while to preserve its battery, so we were each in our bunks in the pitch black when it appeared. A blinking light, a whirring noise. A small messenger drone. Not one of ours. It hovered and made a clicking noise, followed by a message:

Earth children. Your position, compromised. Your fellow man, surrendered. Please exit, leave all weaponry behind. No wish, further loss of life.

The messenger drone retreated from our compromised hiding place. The cavalry was not to arrive. The jig was up. I flicked the heat lamp back on. It made sense that they'd catch up with us sooner or later, probably some form of aerial heat-scanner picked up our signature. I've heard the natives have a reduced body temperature. They've evolved in strange ways, as if they were lichen growing up to smother an observatory telescope, finding a way to cover everything. It's strange to think the first settlers on Mars were human, just like us. How long ago was that? Generations, and lots of them. Whatever happened, happened fast. The people here, if they're even people anymore, adapted rapidly. Physically, mentally, technologically. I suppose the freedom of information act's jurisdiction didn't reach this far, because our guys back on Earth have no concept of what we're up against now. And so it's come to this. Me, Jimmy, Jin, Tomboy and Scraps, trapped like spiders in a jar at the mercy of the big mean kid with more power than he realises.

I looked around at each of them. Solemn eyes to a man. And woman. The inevitability of man destroying man struck me. Even now, I knew how we'd choose to leave this cave. Pride comes before a fall. Until we find out if we can shoot our way out, we'll never know if we could have done it. I have a tattoo. On my inner forearm, something Jin might like. It reads: 'Our world is a cracked bell that no longer sounds'. It's German. I pulled my sleeve up and glanced at it. Time doesn't fix a wound like that. It only coats it in dust. What are we doing here?

"We've got options. Two, I'd say."

"When your foe is standing at the gate, be sure to meet him face to face, for the time of rest is unending," recited Jin, unslinging his beam rifle. I took that to mean his inherent pacifism was to end bloodily.

"What did he say, Jimmy?" asked Tomboy, "the guy in your story, facing the firing squad?"

"Oh, yeah, he said: 'if one has to pass the torch on, ensure they must pass through the flames first', and then we shot him," added Jimmy, hammering the side-screen of his beam rifle and cocking it.

"The closest to poetry you may ever get, Jimmy. Man will always insist those who follow him suffer as he has, thus ensuring progress is limited, finite. It's been a strange but not unwelcome pleasure," said Jin, as he patted a slightly bemused Jimmy on the back.

Tomboy and Scraps rose too. Their hands parted, fingertips slowly disentwining. They unslung their rifles. Scraps nodded at Tomboy and smiled. She smiled back, then turned to the rest of us.

"We're not surrendering to some fuck who calls us *Earth Children*," she said defiantly.

The time for poetry had passed, I gathered.

And so, without having to issue a command, we were ready. No more discussion of what to do. Each person knew how this would end, there'd be no clutching bibles to chests for us, just the inescapable dust of the red planet. Some kind of low, rumbling noise grew slowly, spreading throughout the cave, rattling the stalagmites. We're all facing the tunnel entrance, crouched, ready to see the face of God. Time caught up with us in the end. What are we doing here? What are we doing here?

*

This is the final translated transcript of Corporal Carter's audio-chip recording before it cut out. As you well know, this would usually indicate loss of life. However, due to time discrepancies and technical issues during the campaign, Carter's status remains unconfirmed. This was a strange and vivid account of his inner thoughts and ruminations during what may well be his final hours on Mars. We have drawn together the scraps and conversations into a narrative; as you know, thought-recordings are notoriously disjointed. The findings from the transcript are wholly conclusive. Gentleman, ladies, the situation is irretrievable at ground level. It is therefore the panel's judgement that full nuclear action must be taken against the Martian threat. The freedom and future of humanity is now at risk.

The Light That Never Goes Out

Sat on the comfy seats in the corner of the coffee shop, I was people-watching when it came on. *There Is A Light That Never Goes Out*, by The Smiths. An old favourite of mine. I'd been staring out of the window down at the shopping precinct, watching woolly hats and prams swimming about under a feeble attempt at snow. In my favourite stripy armchair, sat upstairs, I gazed down on the scene, lost in thought. I'd loved The Smiths when I was a teenager. I'd become interested in them through the influence of my friendship group. In fact, this became the time when we all thought Morrissey and Marr were Gods; note the capital G. But *There Is A Light That Never Goes Out* was my favourite. I suppose it was that noughties indie rock boom, and The Smiths seemed the natural originators, or the godfathers of the genre. I could be wrong, better ask a music journalist. Sat here now, nearly thirty, it was this song that most reminded me of those days hanging out together. Which is funny, really, because that kind of group never lasts.

I guess I was closest to Isla and Sally. We three were all in that same sort of grouping, neither strikingly good-looking or overtly bad-looking. Kind of plain. Isla had darker hair, Sally blonde, both quite tall, Sally curvier (her best asset), though Isla had the nicer smile. I was skinny with lank hair pulled across my forehead. And we were not so popular, but not disliked or especially picked on. Stuck in that middle-ish group. Isla and Sally were cousins, by the way, so they had that kind of bond I'd always be external to. But, that aside, we were good friends. I remember it well. Obviously, like I say, it could never last. It just never does at that age, does it?

As if serendipity could read my mind, as I sat gazing down from my favourite chair in the coffee shop, I saw her. Temporarily stopping to adjust the hood of a pram, Sally leant forward, then stood up straight and took in a deep breath. It was her alright. A little older, of course, like me. And a little rounder in the face, also like me (though I had her beat on the facial hair front). I looked on astonished as she turned around, evidently hearing a call, and there, catching up to Sally, was Isla. She was holding a shopping bag. Her hair was different, shorter, a pixie cut, but of course it was her. And I was suddenly seventeen again.

*

A familiar road from a different time and I'm hanging like a Chinese lantern above my younger self. Trees erupted from the pavement as I made my way along, humming a song as I went. I could see Isla locking her front door just up ahead. As it was late summer the evenings still had that lovely clarity and warmth, so we'd taken to going on walks. It was nice to get out of the house and out from under our parents' feet. The summer holiday had that effect – too long at home and you'd feel like a caged bird. Walks were our escape. We'd talk endlessly about the usual stuff: television, films, music, boys she liked, girls I liked. We could speak to each other both rationally and dispassionately, and therefore sensibly, on these things because there was no sexual tension or interest between us. No sexual tension equalled rationality. At least for us, is what I'm saying.

She had her Smiths t-shirt on under a grey cardigan. I wore a striped jumper and skinny jeans. Obviously we both wore converse. Hers white, mine black. We greeted each other with a hug, one of those awkward one-handed ones you do to not get too close, and set off. A few twists and turns and we reached the town park. It could be relied upon to be quiet on a weeknight, bar a few dog walkers. Following its winding paths through foliage and bushes, we reached its centre and the two square ponds topped with algae, crisp packets, and a few jutting bicycle wheels.

"The thing about The Smiths is that Morrissey wrote the lyrics and Marr wrote the music separately, then they put them together afterwards. So no song is alike. See?" Isla said, as if this were the end of the matter. I didn't really want to argue that this in no way dispelled my assertion that some of the songs are a bit samey.

"Okay, okay. I take it back. Anyway. Did you say Sally was gonna meet us today?" I asked, parking myself on a bench by the bedraggled pools.

"Erm, she was going to, but she had to do some work. Listen, you should probably know something," Isla said, staring fixedly at a cardboard box floating on the green water. "Sally kind of likes you."

Unexpected, and potentially quite awkward. We're working a shift together tomorrow night at the pub collecting pots. Why would Isla tell me this?

"Do you like her?" Isla asked, turning to face me, eyebrows raised. I guess she knew my answer already. She always seemed to have an intuition about these things. Every time we talked girls I was into, she already knew who I was going to say. I never once guessed who she was into.

I can hear myself and my thoughts, slipping back into how we used to talk, the same idiosyncrasies.

"Not like that," I mumbled, turning away and taking my turn to stare at the disgraced former box upon the mulchy water of the pond. "What should I do?" I looked left, but past Isla. A little further away I could see and hear a dog running around, its owner flinging a tennis ball about for it to chase before obediently returning it. So simple.

"I would ignore it for now. She goes through these phases. Usually it'll go away when the next one comes along… Talking head-on isn't a good plan. Sally can be a little… oversensitive. I doubt she'll bring it up, she'll just be a bit quiet around you for a bit. So try to act normal, got it?" Isla said, grinning at me.

Act normal, she said. Funny, I thought it'd be quite easy at the time.

*

Nothing happened the following night. That is, not during the shift itself, which passed without event. I thought it had gone smoothly enough. Sally had talked about a gig we should try to get tickets for and laughed about the time I'd worn a coat to my first gig and nearly melted in the mosh pit. We'd laughed, she'd laughed, and we'd got on with the work. A normal night. If Sally and I finished at the same time, as was the case this night, I'd walk her home. Probably out of some code of chivalry instilled by, I don't know, my dad, television, films, local crime rates. It grew colder as we walked. I distinctly recall there was a real chill in the air. A stark contrast to the evening before, as if the weather had mirrored the tension within me. Isla's words of warning from the previous night flashed in my mind as a big neon sign. Sally had a big parka coat on and the furry hood pulled around her. Her face looked like a rabbit's, nuzzling its way out of its warren. I didn't say this, if that's what you're thinking. Even at seventeen I wasn't *that* bad at talking to girls.

"I don't know if you noticed, but I was a little quiet tonight," she said.

Car headlights fizzed past us like flaming baseballs pitched by a pro. The stadium was empty; it was just Sally and I. As we turned off from the main road and kept walking, the engine noise died down and quiet engulfed us. It felt like thousands of empty seats were staring at me and I didn't know why. Unsure how to respond, I waited for Sally to continue. Am I being told off for not noticing? I guess perhaps I'd been quiet myself and she'd picked up on it. She lowered her hood and I could see she was close to tears. As an automatic reaction, I placed a consolatory arm around her shoulders and pulled her in a little closer. We could feel each other's warmth through our coats.

"It's just… Isla and the others. They've been a bit off with me. And then… the other day I heard them talking about me. They were being so mean. Calling me dramatic and silly and all sorts of other things. I felt so horrible. I've been avoiding them for a few days now." Sally stopped walking and pulled me into an embrace, her face nuzzled against my chest. I could feel the vibrato of her breathing and sobbing. I still didn't know what to say. Confusion was my first feeling, and then sadness. And then a little anger too. I remembered Isla's words, calling Sally 'oversensitive', and suddenly saw it in a different light. Not simply a warning to me to be careful about her liking me, but as an insult, an assertion of her weakness. I held Sally a little tighter. Why hadn't Isla spoken about this with me? This was my first thought, and I was a little offended. But this was one of those things I'd not been able to appreciate at the time, that I wasn't entitled to the machinations of Sally and Isla's relationship as both friends and family.

Once we disengaged, we set off walking again and a faint trickle of rain began. We passed the high hedges of the far side of the park and took the adjacent alley to cut through, leaves fissuring underfoot. We reached the end and, hidden by a grey-slabbed wall, was Sally's house. She stopped quite deliberately before we stepped into view of her home and hugged me. In this state we lingered, uncertain, and warm from the walk. Slowly, Sally's head came round and she started to kiss me. I was unable to stop her and, once she'd started, I was unable to stop the kiss from continuing. I didn't want to hurt her feelings and, to add a layer of guilt, I didn't want to stop it because I was kissing a girl and her tongue felt quite nice. So there we stood, kissing surreptitiously like lovestruck criminals, avoiding the gaze of her home the way lots of young couples do. But we weren't a young couple, nor were we mutually lovestruck. Eventually, the embrace came to an end and she stepped away, smiling, victorious. I smiled back because I didn't know what else to do. She said goodnight, walked around the corner, and was gone.

I turned and walked back the way I'd come, cold night air entombing me with a confused concoction of emotions.

*

I'd been ignoring Isla's texts out of a combination of loyalty to Sally and avoidance of confrontation. Eventually, she sent me one that simply read:

She kissed you, didn't she?

Not for the first time, I thought Isla needed to think about a career as a psychic. I stared at the text for so long the letters danced before my eyes in some sort of ritualistic taunting. It was Isla's minimalist put-down. Phrasing it as a question when she knew it was true, to emphasise how *I* was the fool and I had fallen right into it. I tried to call her. I rang her about ten times, thinking she'd pick-up. I envisioned my explanation, my pleading finally winning her round, as if it were somewhat charming in a bumbling Hugh Grant kind of way. But she didn't once pick up.

I lay on my bed staring at the ceiling and listening to The Smiths. *There Is A Light That Never Goes Out* was playing. I envisioned the double-decker bus slamming into me. It would certainly solve my dilemma. I'd lost one friend, that much seemed a given. I could keep trying, I supposed, but there's being persistent and there's just pestering. I always wondered whether I should have kept trying. One of the unresolvable questions of my life. In fact, I remember this as one of the lowest points of my young life. Not only had I lost a good friend, but I was seeing a girl who I wasn't really into, whom I'd only accidentally started dating in the first place because she was sad, and I knew I had to break up with her. In short: I'd fucked up.

I texted Sally, grabbed my coat, and set off right then and there.

*

We met in the park. The same bench Isla and I had frequented when we walked together. The dilapidated cardboard box had finally sunk or been fished out by council employees. In its place were several footballs and a green frisbee, the same colour as the layer of algae topping the water. At least the pond was a good source of oxygen because of the algae. It had little else going for it. If someone else pointed this out, I suspect I'd be protective of the place. It's funny how local attachment works.

Sally was wearing her parka again. She sat staring at me as if I'd contracted an incurable disease. Perhaps it was a family trait that they could predict what was coming?

"Is something wrong?" she said sternly, eyes fixed on me. I, however, couldn't hold her gaze and focused on the discarded items in the pond.

"I'm sorry," I said, "but I can't keep seeing you. I just think we're better as friends."

It felt like a cop out, 'better as friends', but it wasn't necessarily untrue. The problem was I knew from here friendship was an unlikely outcome. It was like saying, 'this thing was better in its previous state, but it has evolved into this particular state, and is incapable of reverting back, but must be destroyed nevertheless'. This felt like two coarse a choice of words, so I chose a softer, clichéd approach. It didn't seem to matter, the result would be upset and, although I didn't feel the same way Sally did, I still cared about her. I dragged my eyes from the pond and looked at her. A few tears already tinged her face.

"I don't understand," she started, before hesitating. "I thought you liked me?"

A loaded question. If I break it down into gradations of 'liking', I appear heartless; if I simply answer 'no', I appear heartless. In this scenario, I am heartless.

"I'm sorry, this just seems the best way."

I look away from the immediacy of Sally's face and up to see a lonely moon in the sky, faded and weary, as day transforms into night. I didn't know what else to say to Sally. After working out in my head what to say on the walk there, all of those things now seem too hurtful, or too vague, or too… true. Our words have been so generic, but with a mountain of complexity behind them. This is the true test of youth, working out how to interpret people when they express themselves inadequately. Actually, it's a test that never really ends.

"Fine," she says, standing up and zipping her coat up. She rubs her eyes to dry them and the skin becomes a raw red around them. "I'm sorry you feel this way. I guess I'll see you at work. Bye." And she walked away, around the pond, across the way, and down one of the winding paths among the greenery. I'd go on to watch plenty of people literally walk out of my life, but this was the first occasion and therefore the most striking. I gazed up at the moon and realised how it was, sort of, a light that would never go out. Just as others extinguished around me.

*

As I sit here in my favourite stripy armchair, watching the people go by, I can see these events from my younger life clearly in my mind's eye. The song has ended, of course. Replaced by Bob Dylan. Just as in the same way I'm sure Isla replaced me, and Sally replaced me. And, as crass as it sounds, just as I replaced them, in time. A few months later I learned Sally and Isla had reconciled. Family ties being stronger than anything we had shared. I was external to the ups-and-downs of their relationship, which meant I was disposable. They've moved on from the little town shopping precinct beneath the coffee shop window, laughing, chatting, living. People are good at moving on.

It's easy to speak and think dispassionately and rationally about these events years and years later. It's easy to frame them and reframe them in my mind. It's easy to see ways in which I should have responded. And yet it was a vexatious period in my life, without clarity or, seemingly, purpose. Now, of course, I see the ways in which I was being moulded as a person by inhabiting the environment of youth. It is this I see as the light that never went out, the lessons gained in the stream of time which is my life. Although the group of friends didn't last, their impressions on me did. Not that I wish to sound like I've got it all figured out. If you find the person who does, give them my number, by all means.

Finally, I shift my eyes from the passage of people below the window, drain the remains of my coffee, and stand to leave. The snow is coming down a little stronger, in facile flakes. It's time for me to move on. Back to life, I guess. Pulling my woolly hat on, I stand up and set off.

The Tree Imps

Deep in the dark, dank and murky forests of the world lie secrets. Secrets can take many forms, manipulating and beguiling innocent minds. Shuffling in the darkness, humming their little songs to themselves, away from the devil of civilisation, are the Tree Imps. There are village tales told and folk songs sang of the Tree Imps; tales of how they guide lost travellers to safety from precarious situations, lighting the easiest clear path. It's something they have done for many centuries, as far back as the oldest family histories. These tales have been passed down through generations like family heirlooms, beloved by grandparents. Yet the stories are based on hear-say, not on eye-witness accounts. Folklore says there is a magical song they sing, like the ticking of a clock.

For some, it is the last song they ever hear.

Our story is that of Bjorn, a Scandinavian woodsman. A strong beast of a man with flowing blonde locks and a ferocious beard to match. He wore thick furs and carried an intimidating axe. But his demeanour was demure and peaceful, like a great oak tree. Bjorn had strayed from the dirt path carved through the expansive forests, a cold and densely wooded area. Trees moulded around him, surrounding him like an anaconda around its prey.

101

Working trips in the tempestuous north meant a long journey home, but one Bjorn had made many a time. Yet on this occasion, he had been compelled to leave the safety of the beaten path. Paranoia gripped him, as is its way; the trickle of a distant stream becomes the pitter patter of some malevolent beast's footsteps when a heightened state of paranoia grips. Bjorn felt hope draining away into the strange darkness, yet he was compelled on, the moon and stars watchful above.

On he walked, the forest noises reduced to sparing whimpers, and then a sheer quiet. Pure, cold quiet. And then: a chiming tick tock, tick tock drifted along the air, floating around like a light mist, somehow enticing and welcoming, mellifluous. Bjorn soldiered on, gripping his axe tightly. Soon he noticed them, sat on branches high in the trees, their innocent round faces moving side to side rhythmically and in unison with the continuing tick tock, tick tock. They gathered, lower and lower along branches, until they were eye to eye with Bjorn. He struggled along the path, captivated by these small creatures. Barely a foot in height and a ghostly pale white, their beady black eyes fixed upon Bjorn. Thousands of them, maybe more. Their countenance was blank and vacant seeming. Unbeknownst to Bjorn, the trees began to spread, until he found himself stood in a clearing. The towering trees stretched a natural canopy above, allowing only slim slits of moonlight to filter through the intertwining branches. Facing him, dead ahead, was a decrepit and aged tree, wrinkled and diseased and black, but somehow imperious, tall and strong. Carved into its base was a throne and, sat upon this throne, was a truly horrifying sight.

A grey and white dirty beard, matted with twigs,

insects crawling amongst it, stretched from the wizened face to settle several feet along the ground before him, as if infested by the same magic as Rapunzel's hair. His slender body had submerged into the crippled wood of the throne. Blind eyes, wet, with glazed white pupils, stared straight ahead in melancholy, as if they had never in their life been happy. He cried out, "you there, please, kill me now. With your axe. Please." Bjorn stumbled backwards, horrified. But he found he could not cry out. His voice was already lost in the forest, crying out elsewhere. The man was reaching a pale hand out toward him. What Bjorn could not know was the man was indeed blind. At least, his physical body was. He saw through the thousands of eyes fixated on the tall, strong woodsman stood in the clearing. He saw through the Tree Imps' eyes, for they offered him the privilege. The man had been sat on the wooden throne for more than three thousand years and spoke in an archaic language and dialect that Bjorn could never hope to understand. The old man's life was extended each time a new victim was sacrificed in the clearing to him, the reluctant idol of the Tree Imps; fiendish and malevolent creatures, possessed of a childlike longing for a father figure. The old man was their unfortunate surrogate.

Bjorn turned, his axe raised high, but it was clear to him now there would be no escape. The Tree Imps were melding together, assimilating one another, their tiny bodies forming larger, fiercer beasts, elongated fingers groping for the tall and strong woodsman.

There was no scream. No final hurrah. And no more woodsman.

To this day, the lore of the Tree Imps lives on. In the stories, the songs, the legends, the tales woven by grandfathers and grandmothers, by village elders and cheerful criers. And in each, the nature of the Tree Imps is mistaken. If you do fall upon the path paved with innocent, pale faces, or hear the tick tock of their song, do not follow, for you will not return.

The Lost Boys' Club

I slid the curtains aside to look at the view. It made me uncomfortable. All that empty space, not a soul in sight.

We'd just moved in and there were boxes everywhere. The house smelled of damp cardboard. I had unpacked most of my things; a lonely box sat in the corner. A few of my twelfth birthday cards lay on top.

The house was perched on a small cliff. There was an uneven stairway that led down to the beach, and a clutch of conifer trees behind us. The beach was littered with stones, some jagged and some smooth. I saw a man walking his dog along it once or twice but that aside it seemed a deserted stretch.

My name is Will. I didn't mind moving as I had few friends to leave behind. And I knew why we'd moved; to get a fresh start. My mother refused to say the words aloud because she seemed to think if it wasn't voiced then it wasn't true. The new house used to belong to mum's aunt and uncle, but one had died, and the other had moved to a care home. They'd lived here in solitude for years. Mum didn't like to talk about it. There had been twins, her cousins, but after some kind of accident mum's aunt and uncle had slowly drifted away from the family. My mother never spoke of it, I got the impression she wasn't really sure what had happened to the twins. It had been years since my mother had seen her aunt and uncle, and then the house was offered to her and the timing seemed right. I think if it wasn't such a fortuitous opportunity she might have been more interested in why they'd left her the house. It had been years, after all.

You could tell they'd begun to lose interest in taking care of the place long before they'd left. There were cracks in the cornices and the paintwork around the windowpanes. The skirting boards were chipped. There were even little patches of damp. Small things which made it feel unloved, uncared for. And now here we were.

"We'll soon be settled," my mother had said, sensing my disenchantment.

"I doubt it," I'd mumbled in reply.

It had rained for days after we arrived. Sat in my bedroom by the window, I regarded the restless sea as it caressed the coast like one does a silk scarf. The clouds edged slowly across the sky as my mother spoke on the phone. She'd been on the phone a lot the last few days, whilst I'd spent a lot of time in my room. I'd found a tennis ball under my bed and taken to throwing it against the wall.

I glanced out of my bedroom window, searching for any hint of change. I turned back briefly but then looked out again. I could see a boy walking down the steps to the beach.

He was about to pass from sight when he suddenly stopped and turned. He looked straight at me. Or at least I thought he did. I was sure he couldn't see me as the rain streaked down my window. He remained there.

The boy waved.

He stood there and waved at me. I moved closer to

the window and wiped away the condensation with my sleeve. He had gone.

I waited to see if he'd reappear, but he didn't. I thought perhaps I was imagining things. The sudden stop, the turn, the wave. I was sure he'd looked straight at me, but how could he know I was there, looking out? Then I noticed something down on the beach; a light. Not the consistent light of a torch, but a flashing light.

On and off, on and off.

I reached for my coat, though I don't know why. I felt compelled to see who this strange boy was. The nearest house was about twenty minutes' walk from here which, in this weather, was a torrid trek. I padded to the front door. Mother was still on the phone in the living room. I slipped out and quietly shut the door. The light continued to flash.

On and off, on and off.

I ran to the steps and stopped at the top. I could feel the sharp cold infecting me already, despite having run.

At the bottom stood the boy. He was expecting me.

*

I thought my heart had stopped for a moment. How did he know I would follow?

I'd come this far, there was no sense in turning back. I began to descend the stone steps carefully; the rain had rendered them slippery. The bushes to the right were overgrown and stretched over the wall, like slender fingers grasping for me. I brushed against them with my shoulder and they sloshed more water on me. It didn't matter as I was already soaked.

The boy had disappeared again. And the light had

stopped too. The feeling that I'd imagined the whole thing rushed to the fore. A sudden sense of foolishness, like I was a cat chasing shadows. Despite this, I found my feet carrying me onwards.

I could see two boats on the horizon, big twin trawlers. They probably had vast nets scouring the sea right now. The tide continued to struggle up the shore.

I reached the bottom of the stairway and looked about. The boy was nowhere to be seen. Then it happened again, a flashing light, this time further along the beach. The cliff twisted to meet the sea, crashing together like cymbals. There was a clear hollow at the base, a chasm that the sea flowed into.

At the base, coming from inside the cove, the light continued to flash.

On and off, on and off.

I began trudging in its direction. The sand had thickened in the rain to the point it had become tough sludge. It had infiltrated my shoes; my feet were freezing. But still I carried on walking, the cliff looming dauntingly to my right, judging me in silence, wondering what drove me on. I couldn't answer this question.

I reached the entrance quickly; the cold has a tendency to hurry you along. The light had stopped flashing when I was halfway along. It seemed to cease once it knew I'd made up my mind to follow it. Unless... perhaps it would stop once its mesmeric quality had hooked its victim? I couldn't say for sure as my feet carried me forwards. I wondered for a moment whether my mother had noticed I was gone. I knew this expedition was foolish, and I didn't wish to worry her, yet I had no desire to turn back. Not yet.

The rocky archway looked like the mouth of some

long extinct sea beast. And I was walking right on in. I was relieved, however, to get out of the rain. I wiped my face on the drier sleeve of the jumper I wore under my jacket and pulled down my hood. Water was still running down my face – pale, red-nosed and red-eyed, fringe plastered against my forehead.

I walked deeper into the cave. My footsteps echoed along with the incessant dripping of water. Up ahead I could see another light, but this one wasn't flashing. It flickered and glowed orange. Someone had started a fire.

I approached cautiously, though I didn't know why. Whoever was there would already have heard me coming. I crossed into the breach of warmth from the fire and looked around. There were three boys, all about my age, sat on the more comfortable bits of rock, all staring at me. There was a ghostly pallor to their skin, like all the colour that once brightened their faces had faded away like morning mist.

One of them stood up. It was the boy I'd followed in the first place. He held a torch in his hand. He turned it on and illuminated his own pale face.

"Hello, Will. Welcome to The Lost Boys' Club."

*

I suddenly wanted to be anywhere else but my legs refused to move. The shadows were dancing across the walls, enraged by the fevered flames. I couldn't concentrate. The sea air had made me light-headed. I shook myself into the present.

"The Lost Boys' Club," I repeat, staring at the boy who'd spoken. He flashed the torchlight in my face.

"That's what I said Will, I can say it again, if you like?"

he replies, turning the torch off. "Sit down."

I picked a place and sat. The rock is cold, and it shoots through me like icy water is flowing through my veins. The boy has stood up and is pacing back and forth, turning about curtly. He looks frustrated. The others sit there quietly. I realise they're very alike, twins probably. They aren't even looking at me. Their attention is on the other boy like soldiers waiting for an order.

"Will, you've come to us at an opportune time, we're soon going to have an opening," he says brightly, placing his hand on one twin's shoulder. He doesn't seem to notice the hand there. The twins continue to ignore my gaze, as if they were seeing the world differently, seeing things I couldn't floating about around us. I refocus on the boy speaking.

"I don't understand, who are you? How do you know my name?" I say. My voice shakes, a mixture of cold and fear.

"I asked those very questions myself once, we all did. And now it's your turn. I'm Michael. And you, Will, are my replacement!" He laughs chillingly and it echoes around the cavern, cutting through the air like a scythe.

"Replacement?" I mutter. What for?

"Those are the rules, Will! Once a boy is lost, he must find someone to take his place, or he's lost forever. That's what happened to these guys, their time ran out and now look at them. Not here, not there, stuck somewhere in between," he says, sneering at the other two. I feel a small flit of sorrow for them. It's only now I see how indistinct they are, almost like tracing paper.

"What if I choose not to?" I say.

"Not up to you, Will. I say so, not you!" he says, pointing at me. He looks strange, like his edges have become less defined, almost blurry. He strides toward me. "For too many years I've lingered, empty and devoid of purpose or life. Everyone I once knew is probably long gone. Do you know what it's like to dangle from a line between two certainties, Will? That is the state in which I have festered for decades. You only get the length of time your natural life would have run for. Once that's done you end up like the twins here, permanently faded, jaded, and forgotten. That isn't going to happen to me, Will, it isn't."

I refuse. This isn't real. I won't be lost like these boys, nothing but a sad memory, physically erased from the world.

I struggle to my feet, fighting against whatever invisible chains hold me to the spot.

I see Michael's face change. He stops. He's no longer laughing, nor does he look like a young boy. His pale features contort with rage. His eyes burn red. There's a clap of thunder outside and the cavern groans. I turn and run.

"It's too late!" he screams. The whole place seems to shake, disturbed by some supernatural rupture.

The echo chases me out of the cove, burning my ears. I run straight out into the rain, not stopping to pull up my hood. It's still beating down, bludgeoning the cliff and beach. The sky is a deep grey.

I keep running, struggling through the heavy-going sand. I look out to see the ships. They've sailed a little further out to sea, still trawling no doubt.

I stumble and fall. I thought I saw, in the water… No, it couldn't have been. I scramble to my feet. The cliff stares imperiously down on me. I look to the heavens, wishing to whoever's listening I'd stayed home. Then I see them. The other lost boys, the twins, sat on the edge of the cliff gazing out to sea.

They turn in unison to stare at me. They're crying. This doesn't make sense.

I run. I run as fast as my legs will carry me. Tears are streaming down my face too, my heart pounding, barely contained within my chest.

I skid to a halt at the bottom of the uneven stairway. Puddles have formed everywhere; I have mud halfway up my jeans.

I look to the top.

Michael stares back down at me.

He was expecting me.

*

He's descending the steps, eyes fixed on me.

There's another clap of thunder, and a first flash of lightning. Even from here I can see his eyes are a burning red, like rubies set in granite, like the golems of Jewish legend. The rain continues to pour.

"I told you, Will; it's too late! I decide my fate, and I decide yours!"

This is it. Whatever it is, this is it. He's halfway down, the overhanging trees flailing beside him in the wind. There's another voice but I can't make it out clearly. It doesn't matter now. Just like the cold doesn't matter or the wet mud and sand clinging to my trouser legs. It's insignificant, like the single bat of an eyelid or a lone droplet of rain.

"It won't even hurt Will, I promise," he says, spreading his arms. For a moment, I think I see a flicker of regret on his face, his last shred of humanity briefly exposed.

But it's just that: brief. Lightning flashes once more and I see his features clearly, no trace of humanity left. Just a cold, sneering, evil mask.

"It won't hurt," he whispers.

I can feel it draining me. Whatever unnatural power this is, it's seeping into my bones, my flesh, my soul. I can no longer feel the cold or the wet and I am incapable of moving. I close my eyes. I think I hear that voice again, still distant, but closer, and it feels oddly familiar.

Another clap of thunder disturbs my reverie. I wonder if it's over yet.

I shudder because it's still so cold. Mist has drifted inland, the air tastes thicker, heavier than before. This isn't right... I can feel the excess weight of my sodden clothing, the water tracing down my face, the filth clinging to me.

"What are you doing!?" Michael shouts. I open my eyes, and trip backwards off the bottom step.

The twins are stood between Michael and I, emitting an ethereal glow. Whatever is happening, Michael isn't winning. I feel everything, I feel the pain in my arms and back from landing on the hard ground. I feel the bitter air on my skin.

"No," he yells, trying to push through the barrier between us, "my time is up! This is it!"

"No more, no more," comes the reply. The words reverberate, like a hymn in a vast cathedral, almost forcing Michael backwards.

"Move!" he screams, launching himself towards me.

"NO MORE!"

The roar is deafening. Michael crashes into the twins,

and it's like the thunder has sounded in my own head, an explosion of pain. The light is too bright, like I'm staring at an eclipse. I close my eyes again and shield them with my hands.

A moment comes and goes. I risk lowering my hands, expecting to see Michael staring down at me. There's nothing before me but an uneven stairway. I realise I'm lay in a muddy puddle, sore and bruised, trying to blink away the rain.

My vision is a little blurry, my hands too wet to bother wiping my eyes. I look up and see a figure descending the stairway.

"No, please," I say, hauling myself to my feet.

"Will," says a voice. A familiar voice, a concerned voice. "Will, what's going on? Are you okay?"

I'm on my feet, shaking violently. It's my mother. I'm safe, safe at last. She wraps her arms around me. I can hardly find the words. I'm shivering too much to talk. She begins to ease me up the steps.

"Let's get you inside," she says, "what the hell you were thinking I just do not know." She's talking to herself, or thinking out loud, one of those things that parents do.

We're at the top of the steps. I look down, expecting to see a boy stood at the bottom, watching, waiting.

There's no one there.

I breathe freely for the first time in what feels like years.

Upon seeing the house again, its former inhabitants come to mind. For a moment I picture it in the summer, sun beating down upon it, the garden flowering wonderfully. Two boys, twins, are playing in the front garden. A sharp tug from my mother wakes me from this brief reverie, and I'm faced with a bleak, rain-soaked building, devoid of joy. Joy it once held.

My mother pulls me onwards and I just want to get indoors, to feel the warmth of the fire, to curl up and have a hot cup of tea and maybe a few biscuits. The things that can make one feel at home, to begin forging a connection with the place. I stumble through the gate and up the path. Mother fumbles for the key to open the front door, finds it, and unlocks the door. I step forward gratefully, glancing over my shoulder. I freeze.

A boy is running down the steps. He disappears from sight.

Signology

Fran unlocked the door to her apartment and, as usual, dropped her shoulder-bag and walked straight to the window. Often, she stayed until close at her restaurant.

The time is 01:07.

Across the street stood a large grey-stone building, easily twenty storeys, comprised of dated offices. Windows stretched around the building, partitioned by equidistant grey trim. Stood inside her apartment, she gazed up at the thirteenth floor. There it was again. A single office remained lit. A lone star in the night sky. For the thirteenth night in a row she stood looking at this light and wondering what espionage or secret double-dealing was afoot. Before this thirteen day stretch, the offices had been a blanket of darkness, bereft of life, benign. Fran couldn't imagine a legitimate reason for the light.

The time is 01:16.

It was dark enough in her flat for the elegant dance of light and shadow to create tension, nervousness.

And then there came a knock on the door.

A firm tap, tap, tap.

Remaining by the window, her eyes flitted from the front door to the solitary lit office on the thirteenth floor.

What was happening in there? Was anything happening in there? She held her breath, hoping the knocker would go away. It was not an appropriate time. Surely she hadn't drawn the attention of the person responsible for the lit office?

The time is 01:23.

And then a duality of collision.

Her door shook as though battered with a hammer, boom, boom, boom.

And, through the window of the lit office, something flew, something solid. Glass shattered and fell as elongated crystalline shards. The solid something plummeted to the concrete street below, which proved equally as solid. This act of defenestration was thirteen days in the making. Fran was frozen, petrified of moving, as if movement would confirm her ongoing existence, witness to such an event. She looked up toward the lit office and then down to the street. In the darkness, the thing resembled a crab, limbs splayed. She daren't turn to go and answer the door. This would be tacit acknowledgement of the existence of the knocker at the door.

The time is 01:27.

Feet fixed in place, her hand touched the cold window, her face so close her breath created a small circle of steam which faded quickly. The thing in the street remained unmoved, dead. For it had to be dead, whatever it was. The assumption it was a finite being seemed logical, although Fran had no evidence beyond its unmoving form down on the solid pavement. And then came the knocking, the pounding, nearly shearing the door from its hinges.

She looked from the still-lit office, to the dead thing in

the street, to her front door. Something lurked behind it. Something with a poor sense of timing or a perfect sense of timing. Feet thawing, she took a step towards it.

The time was…

*

Fran was the intended witness of the defenestration. She'd spent thirteen nights staring at the light of the single office, curious. Business hadn't been going well. The thing in the street had disappeared by morning light. She had chosen not to follow.

The Inventor

Though I could not agree with his self-imposed solitude and subsequent exile, I could understand it. His intellect forced him away from childhood friends and close family and caused his introversion; a condition which would ultimately cost him his life.

In our small town he had achieved acclaim for his myriad great inventions, created to further both the town's fortunes and his own. But this was also the beginning of his introversion and many, many hours shackled to his laboratory, surrounded by all the instruments of his own derivation. The longer he spent hidden away the more people drifted from his life like pollen on the wind, seeking hospitality elsewhere. First it was just the acquaintances that lost interest in him, that forgot him, but the condition of solitude grew more serious as he strived for the one thing that had alluded him during his career; turning base metals into gold and creating the elixir of life!

The secret of alchemy was the Inventor's obsession and had been for many years after he met the old Gypsy man from the travelling carnival. When it first came to town everybody was interested in its enormous rides with their flashing lights and remarkable sounds, and the illusions in the big top and the great many tamed animals that resembled mythical beasts in their magnificence. But he, however, showed no signs of leaving his work until, after a plea from his wife, he was tempted into visiting.

It was as he had known all along; full of superficial fantasy and deceptions, just like all forms of entertainment. He was about to leave when the old Gypsy man summoned him over with these enticing words: 'You have the expression of a man who could discover the greatest secret in this world.' Naturally, his curious mind led him over to the Gypsy man and it was then he enlightened him with the great secrets of the art of alchemy. It was in this moment that the Gypsy man stole from him the best years of his life. What he did not know, as he never saw the old Gypsy man again, was that every time from then on, when he chose to work on his alchemy over his more relevant and feasible works, the old Gypsy man's wrinkles would recede and his hair would grow back, bit by bit, until he had indeed stolen all of the Inventor's best years away.

This obsession saw the years disappear and with them his wife and children and friends, to the point where he became known as the Crazed Decrepit Hermit and all his life's work was forgotten. He eventually died of starvation in his laboratory surrounded by scraps of paper with strange symbols etched upon each discarded piece. For the 'secrets' revealed to him were merely an elaborate game, designed to tease with predestined 'discoveries', forever engaging the inquisitive mind in a labyrinth with no exit. It was a further seven years before the Inventor's death was discovered and his perfectly preserved body was found in its loneliness, surrounded by cobweb-latticed instruments but no papers, his solitude preserved in such a way it might have been an exhibition in a museum.

For the old Gypsy man, his ageing process began again after the Inventor's death. The moment he discovered the body and collected the papers he felt a deep sadness at the scene before him. As penance, he vowed to dedicate his remaining years to charity for what he considered his terrible crime. And the papers he burned, to forever erase both the evidence of his crime and the temptation and delusion the symbols embodied. The labyrinthine game ended with him and the finality of fire.

The Divide Breached

Marin held his sister's limp and clammy hand tightly, longingly. He pulled the cover over her face and rose slowly from his stool. Their Hostel room was dark, uninviting, and now the scene of a departure.

It hadn't taken long. She'd slipped away once the infection took hold. Marin had seen it before. His mother. Neighbours. Strangers lying in the street. The Fog claimed them all in the end, rapacious, grasping.

today, today is the day we fight back

Marin descended the stairs, grabbed a shovel from the cupboard and used the back exit. The sky was a peculiar gloomy scarlet, layered like an indistinct railway track. A permanent haze dims it and takes the edge off, lingering like a painful memory.

A long, thin stretch of garden lay before Marin, the shrivelled remains of an Ash tree looming over it. The garden was overpopulated. Carved into sectors, a dozen makeshift headstones marked the graves. Dark, dry soil, each making up the little mounds Marin now stood amongst, enveloped the corpses of old friends and acquaintances. Marin shivered and shook himself before forcing the shovel into the ground to begin. Hours passed and darkness descended as he continued digging. In the sky was the faint shape of a crescent moon. Jagged cloud severed the scimitar of light.

Ascending the stairs, Marin stopped to gaze at the filthy mirror adorning the wall: weary, baggy eyes, dirty blonde hair flanking hunger-defined cheeks. The fight was almost gone from him. He returned to the room and wrapped his sister in the bed cover and carried her out.

"Is she gone, Marin?" enquired a small voice. Little Janith had poked her head out of the door to her family's room. She coughed heavily and dabbed at her mouth with a dirty handkerchief.

"She's gone Janith, to a better place I think… Go back to bed, it's cold," Marin replied.

"Will you stay?"

"I can't Janith, you be good, okay?"

"She was a nice girl," she said, hiding her face behind a veil of dark hair. She turned and closed the door behind her.

A funereal, solemn procession down the stairs. In the garden, Marin placed his sister's body into the deep hole and began to cover her over with soil, hauling dirt upon her covered body until it was fully submerged. Marin left no grave marker, nor any message or sign. He pulled a small cardboard package from his right pocket, an old tablet box which was creased and mouldy. On it was the name Frampton Holt and a date long since passed. From his left pocket, Marin pulled a cigarette lighter. He lit the box and watched it burn in his hand, ashes gently blowing away. As the flame neared his fingers he allowed it to drift down toward the fresh grave to burn out in its own time. There was a debt to be paid for this, he thought.

Marin patted down the edges of the grave and walked away. He placed the shovel back in the cupboard and returned to his room, threw a few things into a bag, and turned to leave.

He stopped.

Turning, he knelt down and yanked up a floorboard.

"No turning back…"

The pistol slid into his inside jacket pocket, and he strode toward the door. He didn't look back.

*

The old Brandenburg Gate loomed in the distance under a red sky. Layers of ash and dirt had half-buried it. It was like an antiquated hand plunging into the earth, holding on hopelessly to some semblance of a root. Its columns were patterned with cracks, the golden quadriga long lost – one of the few remaining old-world relics.

Decaying, dirt grey buildings cast a shadow over Marin as he walked the streets. Creaking stairs, flickering lights, wallpaper peeling, damp, desiccated and forgotten buildings. Stopping outside a two-storey Hostel, the wind whipped paper wrappers against Marin's legs. Standing upright, yet visibly failing, like an ageing army officer facing down the despot's firing squad, the Hostel appeared frail before Marin. It's the end of the street and the end of this cross-section of Hostels. Dust swirls beyond, the road running into nothingness. Marin ducked inside.

"What you doin' here?" came a craggy voice, a voice in which decades of painful memories rest. It came from behind the caretaker's counter. Dirty glass, with a semi-circle gap at the centre bottom, divided Marin from the speaker. Marin breathed deeply. The memories hidden in the voice resonate with him. He knows some of them.

Was part of some of them.

"Nice to see you too, Halen," said Marin. A scarred face with only one good eye, the other being pure misty white, examined Marin, disclosing no expression. Bald and unshaven, and wearing a thick, dark green raincoat, he was slightly stooped, like gravity was slowly winning the fight. The man to whom the one good eye and one bad eye belonged was sat in a chair, his body as rigid as an old oak tree but without any sense of the solidity.

"I need a favour."

"Ha! A favour eh? Last time I did you a favour, this happened." He jabbed a finger toward his bad eye, which was weeping slightly.

"You know it wasn't me," said Marin, gripping the counter and leaning toward the glass, urgency infiltrating his tone. "We were nearly in. I could practically smell the shit from that boardroom. I wanted them dead, same as you. You weren't the only one who lost something that day."

Halen rose, his good eye maintaining its stony gaze on Marin, observing him for any hint of untruth. A green, chipped filing cabinet stood behind Halen. He shoved some papers from the table into the cabinet and pushed it shut, turned the key with a scratch, and then pocketed it. His hand sat on the cabinet for a moment, as if he were too tired to move. Drifting out of focus, Halen's eyes seemed to be searching for something, or could see someone standing behind Marin.

"Where's Rosa?"

"I buried her an hour or so ago."

Halen disappeared from view. A door clicked to the right. "You'd better come in."

*

It had been two years. A splinter cell had plotted and carried out an attack on The Council, the unseen, faceless auditors of this post-European meltdown system. An informant had infiltrated their cell, exposing their entire operation. Marin had barely made it out of Colony B4 Central alive. Halen too. And they were the fortunate ones.

Fourteen men and women, including Marin's father, had been executed. No trial. No jury. No judge.

the time for talking has passed and now judgement shall fall upon The Council. Rise up, comrades in arms, and face the dawn of a new era

Marin collapsed into a chair as Halen grabbed a couple of glasses and a murky bottle from the cabinet. The room was small, a lamp sat on a desk surrounded by dog-eared maps and stationery; a patched-up sofa-bed took up most of the rest of the space in the room. Halen poured two drinks and passed one to Marin. Sombre, quiet, he sipped, winced, and then sipped again.

"Is there any movement?" Marin said. His voice waivered, suffering from the prolonged silence and the drink he had poured down his throat.

"You don't wanna go down that route, Marin," said Halen, rising sharply from his seat.

"Rosa's dead, Halen, she's gone. If they'd give us medicine, antibiotics, anything, they could help. But they don't. They tell us they don't work anymore, that humankind built up resistance. I don't buy it and neither do you. I'm going to expose them or die trying. It's all I can do for Rosa now. There's no one left."

"Who says exposing them will even make a difference? Eh? What do those dome-living soulless shits care about the outside?" Halen pulled a handkerchief from his pocket, wiped his bad eye, and then drained his glass of alcohol. Crossing the room, he yanked the curtains shut and dimmed the lamp. He lowered his voice to a conspiratorial whisper. "I remember the war, Marin. And I remember our movement on The Council. Everything ends up the same. You can't keep on fighting, some time you've just gotta accept it's over, and this is our lot. The whole world ain't whole no more, it's broken, splintered, and we're remnants of a lost age. Even you, you were so young. Still are, really, and somehow you're lost with the likes of me." He poured another drink and drank it quickly. There were no photographs or personal items around the room. Just maps and transcripts, old ones, the objects of a mind haunted by what the items represent. A mind doomed to go through the evidence, over and over, to find the mistake. To find the error.

"Please, Halen. I have to try. There's a little bit of hope, boxed up somewhere inside me. I'll never shake it, not now. Not now Rosa is… Now she's not coming back. But if there's a chance of changing anything, I'm gonna be there." Marin's eyes were clear, firm, intent. His voice sounded reinforced by an energy, as if other voices were helping it, lending it their power.

Halen limped toward the door. "Take the bed, you need some sleep. I have a message to send."

"Thanks," said Marin.

Halen grunted and flicked a defeated hand up as he left the room.

Draining the dregs of his drink, Marin lay down on the bed and sleep swept over him like the night mists beyond the gate, out in the arid dead space that was Desert Harm. There was nothing left to dream about.

*

Light seeped through a gap in the blinds, stretching lazily across the room, waking Marin. Voices awakened him further.

"I don't like it, Halen, we've waited a long time for this opportunity, we can't throw the chance away on a risk."

"You ain't got a choice, you're a man down and he's done this before. You won't find anyone with a bigger grudge against The Council than him."

"They've got Phasers, you know, androids, blendin' into the crowds, lookin' like any other man. You get caught by one of them, they don't ask questions, you're nothin' but a memory… You say his sister died yesterday?"

There was a pause.

Marin barged in and the new man turned to him. Unshaven, with bags under his eyes, eyes that were locked on Marin; electric blue. He wore a dust-battered motorcycle jacket over a tatty white t-shirt but had an air of authority and conviction about him. Above the three of them, the fan swirled lazily, dust hovering around it like planets orbiting a star.

"I don't have time to waste," said the new man, "We're moving tomorrow, Frampton Holt head office, The Council's big pharma puppet company. We're a man down, someone got stupid. You don't look stupid to me, but I'm not here to mess around. I can catch you up quick enough if you're as good as Halen says, but the risk is huge… every chance the lot of us get ghosted. Are you in or out?"

it's going to be okay son, listen to Halen, remember your orders. We're about to change everything

The light flickered above the rotating fan blades. Typical Hostel light, uttering a persistent low humming noise. Marin despised what it represented. "These lights are always broken... cheap... replaceable. That's how people are seen now. Me. You. My sister... Yeah, I'm in."

"Okay. But this isn't going to be some hero or martyr mission. We wanna be slick, smoke and mirrors, in and out before they know what's happening, think you can handle it?"

Marin looked to Halen, who remained sat down. He wiped his bad eye with his handkerchief in silence.

"You've got a Colt .25 strapped to your calf, heck knows where you found one of them. The outline is faint but visible. But that's gotta be your secondary. You've no obvious holster so I assume it's inside jacket. Your right shoulder just recoiled slightly, so it's on that side, which makes you left-handed," Marin said, the words flowing as if he were returning to an old hobby or job and finding the muscle memory or repeat behaviours kicks in just the same as they always did.

The blue-eyed man smirked and raised his jacket to reveal a concealed holster. "That still don't prove you're up to it, but point taken. And it's a family heirloom, the Colt. Let's get going." He nodded to Halen and spun sharply, stalking off and pulling his hood up with a jab-like flick.

"Might think you were a talker the way you harped on. Look after yourself, Marin," growled Halen, turning back to the desk by the counter, "and good luck."

"Yeah... cheers." He shifted his belt and tightened his

jacket and glanced upwards. A grey, cracked ceiling, peeling in places, stared back at him.

Outside the wind was strong and shutters banged all down the street like a woeful percussion band. The man nonchalantly threw Marin a gasmask. Parked by the pavement was a black motorbike, scratched and battered like an ageing warhorse, but still determined to keep going and going until its inevitable breakdown.

"What's it run on?"

"Piss and vinegar," said the blue-eyed man, a crooked smile gracing his face. He climbed onto the bike. "We're headed across Desert Harm, you'd better put that on. I'm Faber, by the way. We'll travel fast, ask questions later… ever ridden on one of these?" he asked.

"No," replied Marin as he forced the gas mask over his face. The mask was already clouded, so he wiped the grunge with his sleeve.

"Just remember to hang on tight," he said, pulling his own mask over his head.

Faber kick-started the bike and the furious growl attracted curious eyes from nearby Hostel windows, the tenements oddly vibrant as movement kicked the shadows into life. The vibration of the bike nearly shook Marin off, but he steadied himself.

"Ready?"

"Not really."

"Unlucky!"

The motorbike roared like a great grizzly bear launching itself up on its hind legs. They raced up the street, past the last line of stagnant Hostels, past the decaying remains of the Brandenburg Gate, and out into Desert Harm.

*

The dust storm billowed around them as they crossed the red, arid flatland. It was heavy and humid. Marin could see Colony B4 Central, the giant glass bubble commanding the horizon, sat under dim sunlight. They slowed down and eased into an old lookout station, about half a mile out from B4 Central. The station jutted out of the ground like a bullet in a wall. There was wreckage, and degraded, worn-down structures dotted about the grounds, but the main building remained intact. They parked up on the uneven paving.

A stocky dark figure in a gasmask and thick rubbery jacket and gloves stepped outside and motioned them in. Shutters covered the two windows, its flat stone roof vacant. Dust and sand continued to dance violently in concentrated squalls around them. Marin trooped in behind Faber and the door was hauled shut. Black metal covers slid across the windows on the inside, emptiness echoing around them like that of an abandoned warehouse. The light was dim. A buzzer sounded. Faber gave a thumbs-up and removed his mask. Marin replicated.

"I'm guessin' you know about the railroads, right?" Faber asked Marin.

"Yeah, they still usable?"

"Who's this?" said a woman's voice, a gravelly voice full of rich texture, as if it had inhaled the jagged air of Desert Harm once too often. She threw the heavy rubber garments aside and removed her gasmask to reveal a face like a tanned pit bull.

"Easy Leese, this is Marin, Halen's man. He's gonna fill in."

"If you say so. Know how to handle a gun?" She turned on Marin, holding a combative stance. Marin sensed she was the type of person who enjoyed rattling cages and looking tough. Probably, she was tough. He tried his luck with accepting the challenge.

"Probably better than you."

"Ha! We'll see about that. Come on, let's go," she said, her back straightening and her manner easing. Marin had been right. Retreating to the back wall, Leese crouched down and pulled at a handle in the floor. Marin and Faber followed her down a ladder to a cold tunnel. Rusty tracks were discernible despite the dark. They felt like heavy dust beneath Marin's feet.

Faber passed Marin a torch and hopped off the platform. They set off. The tunnel was long and dark and they navigated it in silence. Marin could see shapes in the darkness outside the light of his torch, beyond its boundary. They twist and revolve before him like twin turbines, before stretching into the distance and streaming away. The machinations of his mind become attuned to the darkness, slicker, sharper. The turbines are encased within a metallic abdomen, which is in turn encased within pseudo-flesh. Bullets rip into the pseudo-flesh, the line of which can be traced toward the barrel of a gun. A gun held by Marin. He is sprinting and scared. As this vision dissipates before Marin's eyes, voices begin to mutter around him, voices Faber and Leese cannot hear. It is as if the darkness is speaking to him because he has known darkness all along. Broken lighting in the Hostels; not knowing whether he would see his friends the next day; his sister sliding inexorably towards darkness and his sheer helplessness. Yes, Marin had always known the darkness. The voices went on, whispering duplicitous words and ominous warnings. Marin gripped his torch tightly. He listened for the sound of shifting rocks underfoot and concentrated on it. The tunnel continued, dark and slender.

get out, abort, abort! Phasers, everywhere. Run, run

They emerged in an alley behind a row of modern commercial builds bedecked with white and black panels. Flashing blue or red lights flickered in a nonsensical pattern like a brain-training game. The air was lighter and cleaner, like it had been run through a grand ventilation system. The atmosphere was different too, lighter than Desert Harm and beyond.

"No time to stand and admire, Marin," said Leese, pushing him forward.

A whirring noise from the hover cars slithered down the gaps between the buildings. It was a snake-like hissing. Marin breathed deeply and snatched at his collar.

"Been a while, has it?" asks Faber, "it can be a bit of a jolt, from one hell to another."

"Something like that… sounds and smells the same. It's eerie, claustrophobic," replied Marin.

They reached the end of the alley, its shadows punctured by the buildings' flashing lights, like small barbs of truth finding their way through the darkness. Faber placed his hand against a panel on the wall. It shone orange, then opened to reveal a keypad. Faber punched in a code and the wall slid open.

The room was dimly lit, and the walls covered in maps, blueprints and photos. Pins with different coloured strings connecting one spot to another adorn the larger maps, but the multitude of holes betrayed the uncertainty the operation was being conducted under. Marin walked slowly, arms folded, looking the walls up and down with great care, the creases in his face lengthening.

Books are scattered about. Old books. Marin picked up a well-worn copy of *1984* and scanned the back blurb. A frayed copy of *The Motorcycle Diaries* lay on a greying sofa. A *Communist Manifesto* with no cover left, and yellowed pages, sat on a nearby chair.

"Dreamers," muttered Marin, under his breath. These books were likely worth a lot of money. Most items of value were passed down through families and outside of the Colony Centres they tended to go unchecked, leaving items of rare value in the hands of people who cannot sell them. They'd likely just be assumed to have stolen them. Marin noticed several pharmaceutical books sat on a shelf nearby and ran a finger along the spine of one. "Where is everyone?" he asked.

we regret there have been immeasurable casualties caused by yesterday's detonation. Jubilation must be tempered with sorrow, for today is a day of victory, victory over the dissidents. Our future is now safe, The Council shall make it so

"Resting up. Got another floor up above. We move in the morning. I'll run through things now, then we'll get to bed, go over it again in the morning. We'll introduce you to the others then too," said Faber, casting his jacket aside. He grabbed some dog-eared files from a desk-top. Leese had crashed down on a couch and tossed *The Motorcycle Diaries* to the floor. Marin's eyes followed the book. He knew what it was to be discarded.

"Okay," Marin said, turning back to Faber, "What have we got?"

*

It was still dark. Marin awoke in a cold sweat. He had

dreamed of a tunnel, a tunnel which went on endlessly. The torch failed and he was wandering alone, feeling the ground with his feet, unsure of his step. He heard heavy breathing. A lamp came on across the room. Instinctively, he rose and walked toward it. Faber was holding his chest, heaving deeply. His breaths become shallower and he looked up at Marin.

"Once in a while I find it hard to sleep," he said, a lugubrious grin upon his face. "You got the same bags underneath your eyes," he added. A flask appeared from beneath his pillow. Faber took a small swig then passed it to Marin, who accepted.

"It's always fragments. Never a linear story. And it feels like you're falling between the cracks. Right?" asked Marin. He passed the flask back and quietly pulled up a nearby stool. Others lay about taking precious sleep.

"You should write that down, man," Faber laughed, "probably three years I've been wondering how to put it since my mother died, then you nail it."

"It hits you around year six or seven. Turns out, it doesn't help. Your mother? The Fog?" Marin shifted on the stool – it's old and roughly hewn. It reminded Marin of Halen.

"You guessed it. Not just her. I've seen a lot of people fall to it. Everyone here now has, that's why we're here. We've all got ghosts. Karis and Lyle lost their kid, Jase his wife, me and Leese too, the whole crew. And there's a fucking pharma company sat in the middle of the most affluent Colony in the hemisphere, right on our doorstep, and it does nothing? I don't buy it. Every day, I think about it, I think about everyone who's died… Shit. You carry this stuff forever, don't you?" Faber asked.

Marin sat silently for a moment. Faber stared at the

flask in his hands. There was room in the darkness for many, many people. It buried you in a labyrinth in which you are blind and helpless and may find yourself wandering forever; dark tunnels leading you into unimaginable places. They each could sense in the other a lifetime of pain, fear and anger. It struck Marin that, when you are blind and lost, only another voice can guide the way. "Yes. In a way. But we have to carry it so others don't have to. That's why people look to you, depend on you. Sometimes it's just impossible to help, but there's always someone out there who could. Frampton Holt. The Council. They could. But they don't. Which is why we have to fight now, to carry it for the others." Marin rose and walked back toward his bunk, unsure whether he was still dreaming.

"Come back," Faber said tenderly.

*

The streets thronged with singular order. Men and women in straight, plain dark suits moved in an inexorable fashion. They each stared straight ahead, wordlessly marching toward their next task. Rare snippets of talk were curt. Hover cars whirred gently, but the noise felt sinister to Marin, as if its peacefulness hid a dark secret. Silver and white high-rise buildings surrounded them, glass phonebooths and sleek lampposts were set at regimented intervals along the pavements. A pure white, panelled building, with a curved roof, and incongruous Corinthian pillars holding the entrance up was visible across the busy intersection. The words 'Frampton Holt' were emblazoned in gold letters across the façade. High gates stood before it. Marin gazed at it. Two other people were beside him, each in plain office dress. Marin's shirt was tight across the chest. He fidgeted with the tie.

"Karis, Lyle, don't get lost when we hit the crowd," he muttered, looking down.

"The Phasers should be on the outer rim of their cover area," Karis added, brushing her braid out from her eyes, "clean route in."

"Should be," muttered Marin, "no carelessness. Watch the footsteps. Heavy, crush the ground when running."

"You know your stuff," added Lyle.

The electric gate was closed but unguarded. People milled across the roads participating in the peculiar collective daze of the urban worker. Faber came around the corner and near-imperceptibly nodded, seemingly to no one. The glare of the sun was strong, as if a magnifying glass were being held above them, or the severe spotlight of an interrogator.

The traffic lights at the crossroads outside the gate turned green. A car beeped incessantly as it surged forward, speeding between the traffic, between the converging roads, and straight toward the gate. People turned around. A glint of metal flashed from the jacket of a man about to cross the road. An explosion followed. A car sat to the left was on fire, but it was vacant. A figure edged toward the gate. People panicked and screamed. The beeping car smashed into the gate outside Frampton Holt. People were fleeing. Each of these things happened in a matter of seconds, leaving little time for an authoritative response. The design was simple: induce panic.

A plain-clothes man sprinted toward the gate and concrete turned to dust beneath him. Lyle pulled his gun and shot the sprinting Phaser through the back of the head. Few people remained in the street, the ones that were stood still, either frozen in fear, or in hysterics, screaming, confused. One saw Lyle pull the trigger and immediately fainted, his head catching the kerb with an awful crunch. The rest scattered like villagers running from an erupting volcano.

Marin, Lyle, Karis and Faber met Leese at the mangled gate. Jase, the man from the car, was crouched to the right, a box in his hand. The door exploded and blew inward, shards scattering, and the sudden noise rejuvenated the screams and shouts, though they were distant now. Both cars were ablaze, the fire flickering in the still air. The plain white buildings surrounding Frampton Holt shimmered like a peacock's plumage.

The group strode into a marble entrance hall. Faber hesitated.

"Where is everyone?" he whispered, "too easy."

"Must be in the boardroom," said Leese, running and checking behind the front desk for signs of life.

"Shit! Shit, shit, shit," shouted Jase, retreating from the front window and turning to them, "there are police everywhere, they knew!" Thin red lights flickered and began to trace rapid lines across the marble hall, as if jousting.

"Down!" screamed Marin as he pulled Faber and Karis with him.

no one else made it back, Marin, I'm sorry. They publicly executed those caught alive. It was a warning. We're done, it's over. The Council are too powerful to resist anymore

Bullets ripped through the glass, shattering it and covering the floor in crystalline shards. Jase collapsed in a heap. Rivers of blood swept through the shards.

"No," moaned Karis. She was staring at Lyle. His

lifeless body lay face down on the cold marble by the now bare window – he hadn't made it down in time either. Only the frames of the front windows remained. She shook Marin off and scurried on her hands and knees across the glass, straight over to the window. Tears eased down her face like satellites falling from orbit.

"Go," she said, reaching for Lyle's gun and pulling her own from its holster, "I'll hold their fire. Up the stairs, to the boardroom, try to salvage something from this shitstorm. It can't be for nothing. It can't."

She fired two warning shots blindly.

"She's right," said Faber, his voice shaking, "we have to try, it's too late to turn back anyway. C'mon… Leese?"

Leese was alive and crawled out from behind the front desk. She was crying too. "It wasn't meant to be this way," she said. Her eyes were vacant, as if they had been introduced to something incomprehensible, something ineffable. There was something else wrong with Leese, Marin felt it viscerally, like a malignant tumour, but he couldn't place it.

"We know," Faber said, hauling her along the floor, "let's go."

Marin followed them to the stairs, keeping low. Shots fired behind them. A volley of automatic fire followed, and it echoed in the vast hall, blowing dust and marble out from the walls. Karis fired another return volley, giving them opportunity to move. They climbed the stairs quickly, and were faced with a tall oak door, dense and regal. There was an ancient language inscribed upon it, but Marin didn't recognise it. Marin gripped his gun tightly, pushed the door open, and headed in.

*

"I'd put those down if I were you," said a harsh, gleeful voice. The back wall was glass and sunlight brightened the room, veiling the faces before them in shadow. Treetops were visible outside, perfectly still, verdant but manufactured. Several guns were pointed at them. The peaceful sunlight bounced off them, as well as the freshly shined desk before them.

"And if we don't?" said Faber, his furious eyes fixed upon the man who'd spoken. He had a round face, and a greatly receded hairline. An expensive but ill-fitting suit, with a flower in his lapel, gave him the look of a failed circus administrator.

"Then you will die slower."

Heavyset, emotionless Phaser guards held their guns directly on the group standing in the door. These are the unshaking, immoveable, unrelenting Phasers, the android deceivers of The Council. Marin hadn't expected them to be here at Frampton Holt's headquarters so openly – they were, after all, a puppet company for The Council, not The Council itself. A despairing cry filled the room, disturbing his thoughts. Marin looked at her. Shoulders shrunken, weapon limp by her side, the life and fight drained from her. "No…" muttered Marin.

they had a spy in our operation the whole time. We never stood a chance, Marin. You shoulda run when you were told to run! I'd still have two good eyes if you'd just listened! It's over Marin. It's all over

"Now drop your weapons and drop to your knees, please. Do it, I don't have time for pleasantries."

Something in his voice was familiar to Marin. The Council announcement from long ago, declaring the execution of the captured rebels, including his father, over the radio.

Each of them complied with his request. They tossed

their weapons aside and sank to their knees. The man turned to Leese.

"Leese, thank you for your efforts," he said. He smiled at her, leaning back and forth on his heels. It was the hollow smile of a bank teller, a smile that faded from view as quickly as it appeared.

"You bastard, you said no one would die," she whispered. Faber stiffened perceptibly, the betrayal sinking in. His jaw clenched, eyes fixed dead ahead.

"Yes, yes, I did. I lied. You see, Leese, I'm a manipulator, it's what I'm good at. It's why I am who I am. And this, this is why you are powerless." He pulled out a gun from within his desk and shot her through the head. Leese collapsed forward. Blood streamed from the wound. The man strolled around the desk spinning the gun nonchalantly on his finger.

"Now, I'm going to allow you one question. I guess I'm just feeling chirpy today. Go ahead, don't be shy."

A bulky file sat open and free on the desk. It was bound in metallic wire mesh. The open suitcase by it had a passcode and fingerprint device along the seal. Faber stood up, his hand brushing his leg as he rose. The man looked perturbed for a moment but allowed him to continue. Faber was unarmed. The Phasers trained their weapons on him.

"I want to know, do you have a replacement for antibiotics, or anything, any drugs to fight the infections caused by the Fog? People in Hostels die every day. If you have it, they need it," he said, and edged back slowly.

"We don't need to replace them. They never ceased to work. They may have, if overuse continued. That's why we pulled the plug. You can't make money from something that doesn't work. But you can, if a global epidemic is declared and you, against the odds, produce a miracle drug and charge a premium that only those who fall on the affluent side of the divide can afford. We've spent a long time building this world. The Council. Frampton Holt. They're one and the same. You rebels, you rallied so long believing some secret lay within Frampton Holt pharmaceuticals. Oh, you weren't wrong, by any stretch, but each piece of information you thought drove you closer to your goals was merely planted by us. If we control the opposition, we control the world. The Council is merely a rumour, a body to deflect anger and rage in some, inspiring control and subordinate behaviour in others. There are so many others like you out there who have no idea they are directing their efforts against a symbolic, metaphysical entity. When a rebel group targets Frampton Holt, we exterminate them, like the insects they are. When they target The Council, they are targeting a concept, an idea of an enemy."

Not content simply with winning, joy was derived from the game, from toying with those beneath you. Marin knew his type – overconfident to the end. He glanced sideways at Faber and, for the first time today, properly looked at him. The outline around his calf didn't resemble a Colt .22 anymore. It was a bulky, square shape. Careful eyes watching his enemies, Marin shifted forward on his knees, edging a centimetre at a time. He'd need to be quick. But in this moment, a darkness threatened to blind him, to rob him of hope.

There was nothing now. Silence. And then calls from downstairs. But Marin wasn't listening to the voices in the here and now. The flashes threatened to overwhelm him, traumatic memories thronging like a panicked crowd of people rushing to a single exit.

the perpetrators have been caught and met with retribution. Executions have been carried out, for there can be no tolerance of violence in a tolerant society. So says The Council

"And I think that's our friends the police. Yes, our friends indeed." The man stepped forward and clapped his hands together, but then hesitated. There was a ticking noise, growing louder. The gaps between each tick quickly shortened, as if rushing to a hasty conclusion.

"Sorry Marin, I hoped it wouldn't go this way, but I needed a plan B," a crooked smile gracing Faber's face as he glanced sideways at Marin. He ran at the man and lunged. Marin remained still, on his knees, head down. The Phasers opened fire, converging collectively on the one-man attack on their boss.

Marin leapt up and made for the window. He grabbed the file from the desk, the ticking now behind him reaching a high-pitched peak, and launched himself through the glass as the boardroom exploded behind him. The force of the explosion blew him further away, but he landed in a bush, crashing through a thinly webbed thicket. Trees flanked the bushes and extended to the walls at each side. Marin stood unsteadily, too quickly, clutching the file to his chest. Thick black smoke was drifting from the building where half the wall was blown away. In the confusion, they won't expect any survivors. He leant against a tree, panting, a sharp pain in his side and his shoulder, but alive. The tree was blocking him from sight, and the smoke was too thick to see anything yet anyway.

Marin blinked frequently, as if blinking blood from his eyes. He was heaving still, but his breath was returning, the pain becoming manageable. A ringing in his ears threatened to exhume memories he'd long since buried, but he clutched the file to his chest. Soon, he'd be okay to move. If he could make it back to the underground tunnel and make it back to Halen, he might just survive. Marin opened the file, read the front page, and smiled. That man had called it a 'divide'. Well, we'll soon see what we can do about that, thought Marin. He limped wearily away, glancing over his shoulder as he went.

The Last Ride

The air conditioning is bust on the coach. Nothing to stave off the unnatural heat, it buzzes incessantly, uselessly. All of the window covers pulled down, brightness of the fiery sun seeping in round the edges. Most people sleeping. A grunted snore followed by a sniffle comes from somewhere behind me. I'm sat by the window, about halfway down, and evidently coping with the heat better than others. The guy next to me keeps adjusting himself in his seat, twitching like the convulsions of a death throe. I lean left against the wall to stay clear.

I'm not sure how long we've been on the road for. The clock up front above the driver's head is bust too, stuck on 00:00. Figures, you get what you pay for.

"Hey, buddy, hey," says the twitchy guy, nodding to the right surreptitiously.

"What?"

"The guy," he adds, his eyes wider. I crane my neck to get a look.

Sat across from us is a young guy, long floppy hair, strapped in tight. He's straining against the seatbelt and clutching it tight. Sweat is pouring down his forehead like it is Niagara Falls, glistening even in the gloom of the coach.

"What's his problem?" I ask, returning to my position against the wall. Another violent snore erupts behind me, this time with a splutter. Sounds like how I imagine bubbling lava does. Additional wheezing.

"You think we should tell the driver?" says the twitcher. He starts fanning himself with a magazine. Always busy, always doing something with his hands, I thought. I begin to notice his pale, grey, pockmarked skin. This one is probably a pothead or an acid freak. I have heard about these sorts.

"Do what you want," I say, closing my eyes.

*

Some more time passed, I don't know how much as I had slept. I realise why I'd awoke. The floppy-haired kid across from me is talking, no, babbling. Not to anyone. Just going on and on. He sees I am looking at him and now the babble is aimed at me.

"Where are we going? I know my rights. I've seen TV. Who are you people? Who are you?" He struggles with his seatbelt again, struggles so hard it must be cutting into his chest, pushing against his ribs. He is frantic, but finally unclasps the seatbelt and stands up. He bangs his head – low ceiling. He continues to shout the same questions, rubbing his head.

Several people hiss at him, making noises of disapproval, shushing at him. The commotion blends with the buzz of the broken air conditioning. He recoils. There is a ding, an announcement.

"*Passengers are reminded to stay in their seats at all times and keep their seatbelts on. Thank you.*" Slow voice, bored no doubt, but authoritative. The young boy succumbs to the call and retreats.

*

I am a park ranger here at Yellowstone National Park: law enforcement side of things. A missing person, specifically a young boy, 14 years old, stripey t-shirt, floppy sandy hair. The beam of light from my flashlight traces the ground like the large luminescence of a lighthouse out on a dead sea. Surrounded by tough terrain, it is a bad place for a young boy to lose his way. There are bears and wolves out here, deeper into the subalpine forest. Running water off in the distance, it sounds like thousands of pinballs cascading down a sloped street. It is easy not to know your way in the dark and slip. Roots rise and fall like torrid waves, or a pit of grasping disembodied hands. Dragged down, carried off. I am surrounded by the wild whistle of the forest under an ethereal moon glow. My radio scratches on, nothing to report.

Lots of people go missing in Yellowstone, it is a dangerous place if it isn't shown respect. Sometimes people go missing and they don't come back. Fall into geysers, think they can swim in them. Not a good idea. This family had been hiking and exploring and pretending they were tracking wild animals. This is the kind of thing people do.

With each step I can feel the forest sloping upward. I can now hear crying, but this is not the crying of a wild animal. My pace picks up, I am the first to happen upon him. Our eyes meet as I stumble toward him, shaking and clinging to a tree. Simple case of taking a wrong turn, panic, run, become lost. That's what they all say.

"You'll be okay, son. I got my radio, and some folks won't be far away. Your mum and dad are worried."

I say this to the boy, still keeping his wide, tear-filled eyes on mine. I grab my radio.

"Tell the parents I got the boy. Ask them how the hell he could wander this far out."

What strikes me, as we begin to edge our way downward, toward the voices, are the boy's eyes. Not the eyes themselves, but what they spoke to me. It was loud and it was clear. There was profound fear, as if in that moment something clicked and he understood the exact meaning of the word, the visceral wrench of your insides. He must have thought I was a grizzly bear. Once he saw me, and saw I bore only a passing resemblance to a bear, he deflated and shrunk into a ball, hoping the world wouldn't disturb him further.

Stars above shine clear here, making it lovely. There is a crunch underfoot. We are hurrying along. Voices are a little clearer. I have wandered a little too far myself. Behind me I hear thuds and a growl that might well be a roar. Vibrations shoot up our legs. Our eyes both have that fear now. Our insides wrench.

"Run!" I say. Keep running.

*

Next to me, the twitchy man plays with bracelets beyond the sleeve of his top. They have various attachments he fondles and thumbs. His eyes rise to meet mine.

"He makes me nervous," he says, and nods at the

young man sat across.

"I'll bet," I respond. My response is the driest thing on the coach as the air is turgid with humidity. Twitchy takes his jumper off, no longer able to stand the heat. His arms are scarred. I turn away. It is a sad case.

"Go on. Look away if you gotta. We all got a past," he says, thrusting his arms at me.

"Past is all we have now, don't you think?"

We could argue longer, but what would be the point. I'm stuck here, he's stuck here. Twitchy's eyes squint, his grey skin bunches across his forehead. He knows it just as I do. Eyes down, back to fiddling with bracelets, his leg begins tapping a rapid, incomprehensible jazz beat. In the seat in front the inconsistent wafting of a fan, faster, accelerating like a motor car; slower, a gentle walk through a picturesque park, free from danger and fear.

I shiver with a start. There is scratching and humming to our right.

Breathing heavy and pawing at the seat, trying to burrow out of the coach, or create some great chasm to sleep in, the floppy haired kid is in another frantic episode. The coach continues on, bust clock, bust air conditioning. A shuddering snore, once more, from behind. I turn to look through the seat gap but cannot see the source. I now look at the boy again. As I do, he stands up and stumbles out of his seat into the aisle. In his eyes I recognise something, a glimmer that flashes like lightning. Fear. It is the same fear I saw in the child, lost in Yellowstone, lost in the darkness of the forest. It is a fear of the unknown, of being in an alien environment, surrounded by strangers, like you're suspended in mid-air. The boy in Yellowstone was engulfed by the unknown. Somehow, this boy is too.

"He doesn't know," I mutter.

Next to me, the twitching stops.

"How can he not? We're on the way there!" says twitchy. Violently, he pulls a bracelet from his wrist, beads tumble to the floor and slide down the coach in a stampede. Angry eyes flash to the young man. His eyes are blind.

"Why won't someone help me?" screams the boy, arms swinging round, flailing like he wants to punch away a horde of bees. Sweat flies from his glistening forehead. A further chorus of boos and hisses, like some gaudy pantomime. An elderly couple in front speak in raised voices. "Youth today," they grumble. I retch. Heat spreads through me like a river that has just broken a dam, searching out nooks and crevices rapaciously. Garish light oozes around the edges of the window covers on both flanks. Evidently, the heat sneaks up on me. The constant buzz of the broken machinery rises to a din.

Heavy footsteps echo down the coach; thud, thud, thud. The driver has had enough and makes her way toward the ruckus. She is tall, robust and Greek-looking. At the front of the coach, on the wall by the bust clock, is a license plate that reads 'Sharon'. It looks to be a Texan plate. I wonder if this is her name. Now I duck my head between my legs, the sickness of the heat crashing over me like a tidal wave.

"Boy I do not get paid enough to put up with your racket," says the driver with a Texan twang. "Sit your butt down and enjoy the ride, I can be sure it's the last one you'll ever take."

The boy lunges at the driver and grabs her by the front of her shirt. Twitchy next to me squeals and throws his hands up to cover his face, anger evaporating. Sharon is a heavy-set lady, and the boy is meek and frail and unhinged so as she shoves him away he flies backward and hits the floor. Sharon looms over him.

"Wait," I say, lurching upward, woozy and nauseous.

"I'm still waiting," she declares curtly. I realise I'm staring at her, leaning against the seat in front. The claustrophobia of the coach reminds me of great galloping forests of trees racing away up a mountain, not from a distance, but from within the heart of it, surrounded by towering ferns and unfamiliar sounds of wildlife. Now I imagine these trees are on fire, collapsing around me, and a child is screaming somewhere unreachable.

"The boy," I gasp, throat dry from the cloying, overused air that has run down it. "The boy doesn't know, doesn't know he's dead." I collapse back into my seat. Pain subsides, buzzing eases.

A hushed murmur spreads throughout the coach, rises to chatter, then silence once more. The young boy screams. He screams as if his lungs are making their last stand in the face of insurmountable odds. Once more he lunges forward, but then slips sideways into his seat. He wrenches up the window cover so sharply it snaps from its hinge and hangs loose, swinging to and thro; covering the window, not covering the window.

"No, no, it can't be. This can't be right. What trick is this? You people kidnap me in the dark, blindfold me, tie me in until I struggle free and what is this hell you bring me to?" he declares, his voice reaching a high pitch before shrinking, shrivelling. He faints, falling into his seat.

The window cover still hangs loose. My head rises and

I see. Cascading walls of virulent orange flame, a river of scarlet red, rushing along as if through a vein. Things are floating in it. Fire, so bright, phosphorescent and consuming, scorching my eyes. I turn sharply away. It is like looking directly at the sun. The driver reaches over and pulls the cover back up fully, manages to hook it up, at least temporarily.

"Unfortunate boy, he'll struggle down here," I hear Sharon mutter. She heaves the boy further up his seat and wanders up front, whistling a morbid tune. The coach hasn't stopped moving. Not once while the driver dealt with the disturbance. A fantastical point I overlook; sickness still bubbles inside me. I see the young boy prostrate across from me, too young to be making this journey. Whimpering next to me, legs up on the seat, head hidden in his knees, twitchy, too young himself, retreats into a protective shell. There is a loud snore from behind. One person remains undisturbed, resting peacefully. I raise my head and look down to examine my wounds, gaping and unclean like a sea trench. I lean against the wall and close my eyes.

Author's Note

You may be wondering what ties this disparate collection of stories together – what brought on the title, 'Condemned To Be'? I should add, there is an irony within the title which lies in it forming the bulk of Jean Paul Sartre's famous line, 'man is condemned to be free'.

Let me elaborate (briefly).

For me, there is a common thread running throughout these stories. It appears more discerningly in some stories than in others, but I feel it is always present. That is the sense of a person trying to make a choice or to act when placed in circumstances beyond their control. Whether this is a man about to lose his job due to technological advances being forced into a poor decision by a perilous financial situation; a freedom fighter with nothing left to live for following the death of his sister; a teenager feeling so caught up in the flow of a romantic situation he is unable to express himself freely; a young woman engulfed by momentous political shifts; or even a woodsman led astray by the lure of magical creatures (okay, I accept this one is a little loose…). Each story places a person or persons in a situation that elicits a choice. The person or persons may, on the surface, choose freely how to proceed. But circumstance is what presents a set of options to a person.

The question then, is this: are human beings truly free?

If one makes a choice and accepts the consequences of said choice, they can be said to have made a free choice. But if a situation dictates a set of options and a person chooses the most agreeable of them, what does that say for the ultimate freedom of a human being? For what it's worth, I'm not certain the stories (or the author, for that matter) fall definitively either way.

Beyond the questions I hoped to raise with this collection of genre-hopping oddities, I also hope you enjoyed reading them. I certainly enjoyed writing them.

Until next time.

About the author

Stephen Howard is a British novelist and short story writer born and raised in Manchester, England. He was always an avid reader but finally decided that, aged twenty, perhaps he too could write stories people may enjoy. This eventually led to the self-publication of his first novel, *Beyond Misty Mountain* (2013), inspired by an enduring love of Terry Pratchett's *Discworld* series.

Since then Stephen has completed his Bachelor's degree in English Literature and Creative Writing with the Open University, gaining First Class Honours, alongside full-time employment working in marketing, then in elderly care, before settling into local government administration. During this period Stephen has had short stories published on The Flash Fiction Press website and in the Tigershark Publishing ezine.

Outside of writing, Stephen supports Manchester United and tries to get to Old Trafford when he can, although he does enjoy watching the match in the pub. He can also be found taking pub quizzes too seriously somewhere in the Urmston area – you may even have caught his brief appearance on Mastermind in 2017.

Printed in Great Britain
by Amazon

34726354R00095